THE
LAST
RIDE

THE LAST RIDE

Carolyn Haddad

DODD, MEAD & COMPANY
New York

1   2   3   4   5   6   7   8   9   10

Library of Congress Cataloging in Publication Data

Haddad, C. A.
   The last ride.

   Summary: On his first date with popular Cindy, high
school sophomore Doug refuses to let her ride in a car
with a drunk driver, but later, after a fatal crash, he
feels guilty for not having somehow saved the car's
other passengers as well.
   [1. Drinking and traffic accidents—Fiction.
2. Traffic accidents—Fiction.   3. Death—Fiction]
I. Title.
PZ7.H116Las   1984   [Fic]   84-10113
ISBN 0-396-08458-3

For Ben and Judy

1

Between second and third periods, between science and math, Doug Valvano caught Cindy Ballentine in the hall, gathered up his nerve, and asked her to go to the Snow Ball with him. To his surprise, she accepted. "You will, really?" he said to her, betraying his expectation of defeat.

She looked at him a moment, then smiled. He grinned in return. Really. Cindy Ballentine was going to be his date. While she slipped into her English class, he had to run down the corridor to make it to math before the final bell.

"No running!" Mr. DuBois shouted from the door of his French classroom. Doug barely heard him. Teachers had been telling him not to run since kindergarten.

Doug slid into his seat as the final vibration of the bell subsided. The page number of the day's lesson was written on the board. He was expected to have his book open, his math notebook turned to a clean page, and a sharpened No. 2 pencil in his hand. He was accomplishing all this when Sam Rosen leaned over from the next row. "Did you ask her?" Sam whispered.

"Yes."

"So what did she say?"

"Yes."

"You lucky dog."

Doug wrote down everything Miss Futron told them to write down. Yet trigonometry was the farthest thing from his mind. Cindy Ballentine, *the* Cindy Ballentine, had accepted ordinary Doug Valvano's invitation to the Snow Ball. It wasn't like last time, not like the Turkey Trot before Thanksgiving vacation when he had asked Valerie Brown, and she had told him she was waiting for that jock, Pig McKennah, to ask her. But if Pig didn't ask, she would consent to go with Doug. Well, Pig did ask Valerie, and after that, what was the point? Everyone knew he had been rejected.

Was it his charm? he wondered. Was that what turned Cindy on to him? He considered their relationship. It had begun to build to this resounding crescendo during football season. He was in the band. Second trumpet. Cindy was on the pom squad. Just after the halftime show it was the pom squad girls who opened the boxes of apples and delivered them to each band member. Cindy always made sure he got a nice red one, now that he thought back on it. At the time he had been too enamored of Valerie Brown to notice. Valerie Brown, junior-varsity cheerleader, top of the pyramid, the "I" in Wildcats. Valerie and Pig, junior-varsity football captain, now an item around school at Doug's expense. And all the time Cindy had been waiting for him to come to his senses.

Then football had faded into basketball at Oakdale High and the band was relegated to practicing for the annual winter concert. But Doug and his friends would go to the basketball games on Friday nights, where Valerie had been demoted to the Wildcats "D" and where Cindy Ballentine shook her red and white pompons with such fury that Doug rose from his seat just to watch her.

At the dances after the Friday games, Doug regretted that he hadn't taken up his mother's offer of dance lessons. He hung around the walls, sort of circling, wondering if he would have the nerve to get out on the dance floor and make a fool of himself, wondering if he would ever ask some girl to make a fool of herself with him.

Fortunately, he didn't have to. Cindy asked him to dance first. It was a Sadie Hawkins' number. She was still dressed in her red turtleneck, her white skirt, and her saddle shoes. "I'm not really good at this." He tried to apologize even before he reached the dance floor.

"No one is," she assured him, as she grabbed him by the hand and pulled him forward.

He jumped, he swiveled, he hopped. He tried to match Cindy's moves. But she was a pom squad member and he was only second trumpet.

The dance was over. They stood facing each other. The next record plopped onto the turnstile. Something by Diana Ross. "May I?" he ventured to ask.

Cindy floated into his arms. Her hair was fresh and clean, smelling of lemon. He tried not to step on her toes. When the dance was over, he knew he would somehow get up the courage to ask her to the Snow Ball.

2

Cindy Ballentine sat across the lab table from her best friend, Michelle Tourney, whom she had known forever. They were supposed to be making slides from onion skins, but, to them, biology lab was always an opportunity to converse, an opportunity they rarely missed out on.

"Are you really going with him?"

"He asked me, and I said yes," Cindy confirmed.

Michelle shook her head. "Why Doug Valvano? He's such a nothing."

"He's sort of cute. He's shy and quiet."

Michelle couldn't accept it. Her best friend was wasting herself, throwing herself away on someone who didn't count. What kind of date was Doug Valvano for the Snow Ball? "Isn't this a rather heavy price to pay just to get back at Charlie Sims?"

Cindy was using a single-edged razor blade very carefully. Still her slices came out too thick.

"Cindy?" Michelle demanded.

Cindy preferred not to answer. Maybe she had had enough of Charlie. She didn't know. Maybe he was too old for her. He was a senior, after all, while she was a sophomore. Oh, she liked the prestige of being seen in the halls wearing his football jacket. But she didn't like the way he pressured her on dates. She wasn't going to do everything he wanted. She didn't want to be his girlfriend that much.

Last week, as if to spite her, Charlie had asked Lisa Nevins out on a date. This week—well, maybe she was retaliating by accepting Doug Valvano's invitation. But she didn't think he was as drippy as Michelle did. He was nice, sweet, smart.

Oh, Cindy knew all the unwritten rules at Oakdale, how pom squad members and cheerleaders were only supposed to be seen with jocks. But one date outside that tight circle didn't mean she would break the rules forever.

"How are you going to get there and back?" Michelle, ever the practical one, asked.

"I don't know. Maybe he has a friend who drives."

"Hah. He hangs around with all those sophomore grinds."

"Well, at least a sophomore grind would be able to find an onion cell," Cindy said, exasperated. Her onion lay chopped up and her tear ducts were overflowing from the vapors.

Mr. Backley hurried over to Cindy. "What have you done?" he asked almost frantically. "Are you making a slide or are you making relish?"

The class giggled while Cindy blushed in humiliation. With one swift stroke of the razor, Mr. Backley cut her a slice of cells. He slid them onto the slide and placed the circular protective seal over them. "Now see if you can draw the cells," he said to her. From the look he gave her, she knew her mark for lab work was not improving.

She positioned herself over the microscope while Michelle whispered to her. "Maybe you can come with us. I'll ask Red if he has room for you."

Cindy considered it. Michelle was going steady with Red Bucknell, varsity halfback on Oakdale's football team. She didn't really know how he and Doug would fit together. But then, wouldn't riding with Red be better than having to be picked up and dropped off by Doug's parents? That was rather demeaning for high school. "You can ask Red," she acquiesced unenthusiastically. Then she turned the focus on her microscope and tried to adjust it to her eyes. The cells were there. They had to be. Somewhere.

Doug Valvano walked home on a cloud, unaware that he had been the object of such critical discussion in biology lab. He assumed that everyone in school was as happy as he was that Cindy Ballentine had accepted his invitation. It was the first time since he had come to Oakdale High that he had felt supremely confident.

It had been a shock, high school. Especially after the years at Kennedy Junior High, where his sister was a seventh grader now, where life had been so simple. Good friends, good classes, no pressure. Here at Oakdale, it was hard to know where you stood, the school was so totally divided into the ins and the outs. The ins—like the jocks, the cheerleaders, the pom squad. The outs were the rest of them—like himself, Doug admitted—outside the flames of the sun, only basking in reflected glory. At least that's the way it looked from the perspective of a newcomer like himself. A sophomore. The lowest of the low.

That's why it was so remarkable that Cindy Ballentine had agreed to go to the dance with him. She of the golden circle. Now he would have to try to make the evening perfect for her. Which was going to be hard right off the bat, since at fifteen he couldn't drive. Legally at least. He could almost taste the day when he turned sixteen and could get his permit, then his license, and then—freedom! But now, for the Snow Ball? Doug supposed his only option was to ask his father, maybe convince him to dress up like a chauffeur? No. He didn't think so. Hey, maybe Sam would ask someone and they could double date. He'd speak to Sam about it. Try to convince him that the risk of rejection was worth taking.

And if Sam didn't? Well, then, Doug would be alone with Cindy on his first date. Not a party at someone's house. Not a pep rally. Just he, alone, with Cindy. The two of them, together.

He had to be cool. He had to be collected. He had to do the popular, the right thing. He didn't want to do anything that would spoil this one date in a million.

3

Kara Valvano sat at the kitchen table doing her English homework. Every now and then she glanced across at Willy Nathan, supposedly doing his English homework, too. They had struck a bargain when they entered Kennedy Junior High last September. Kara would help Willy with his English and social studies if he would help her train for cross-country and the spring track season.

Ever since she could remember Willy Nathan, he had been running, either to get to school on time or to get away from school. Now he ran for the sport of it. He dreamed of the Boston marathon, even the Olympics.

"Willy?"

"Just a minute, Kara." He hunched closer to his book.

Willy had fulfilled his part of the bargain, she thought. They trained together every day. She could feel herself improving. She could even endure the teasing of her girl friends about Willy, because those girls dreamed silly dreams, like meeting a rock star. She fantasized about marching in the Olympic parade alongside Willy and then winning a gold.

"Willy?"

"In a second. Honest."

She sighed. She really tried to help Willy with his studies but Willy, when he wasn't running, always had his nose stuck in a book. Not just any book—thirty-two books. The "Pretender" series, Numbers 1 through 32, which Willy had taken up after his parents announced their separation. Kara had seen all the volumes pass through Willy's hands. He had the thirty-second before him now. What did he see in the hero, Lance Dupliscis, double agent, supposedly working for the Bulgarians but actually working for the CIA—or was it the other way around? Even the covers were silly: A man plunging through a wall; a man stopping a car with a flame thrower; a rather revealing female form with a gun always in the background.

"You'll rot your mind," she warned.

Willy's eyes flashed upward at her. "He's about to be mistaken for an East German."

"Is that serious?"

He flipped the open book down on the table. "Don't you know anything?"

"I know English. That's what we're supposed to be doing."

"Theirselves, themselves; good or well; between you and who? Why can't we write the way we talk?"

"I bet Lance Dupliscis had to learn grammar when he studied all those foreign languages."

"Lance didn't have to study foreign languages, Kara. I've told you before. Lance's father was a German who lived in Bulgaria; his mother was an American who lived in France. Then when they died halfway through the series, he was adopted by an Arab sheik who married a Greek patriot. Lance came by his languages naturally."

"I still can't understand why he was adopted when he was in his twenties."

"That's because you don't understand international espionage."

"And you do?"

"You'd be surprised by how much you can learn from traveling with the Pretender."

"Obviously not English, since you practically failed your basic skills test."

"The apostrophe is dead, Kara, face it. And the semicolon? Who are they trying to kid?"

"Whom."

"Are you going to grow up to be a teacher like your mother, or a runner like me?"

"I thought you were going to grow up to be Lance Dupliscis," she teased.

"Well." He leaned back in his chair. "Runners do go to a lot of meets overseas."

"Oh, Willy." She gave up.

"All right," he conceded. He grabbed his workbook and opened it with annoyance. "Page seventy-nine?"

"Right."

"Okay. Here goes. I don't feel so good."

"Why, what's the matter, Willy?" Kara's mother asked, as she came into the kitchen with dishes from last night's living-room binge.

"English," Willy replied.

"Ah," Mrs. Valvano said, understanding. Her nose crinkled. "Have either of you washed lately?"

"Mom! We're in training."

"Personal hygiene is nothing to be frowned upon."

"What should I do? Leave Willy sitting here while I run upstairs and take a bubble bath?"

Her mother smiled, trying to hide her irritation. "I appreciate the need to train in all sorts of weather. But let me put it this way—you two smell like wet dogs." Exit mother.

When Mrs. Valvano was safely out of earshot, Willy said, "It must be awful to have a mother who's a teacher."

"Not really. Except when I tell her how much I hate some of my teachers. Then she says things like, 'Well, have you ever considered how they might feel about you?' I hate the way she can see both sides. Anyway, we're fortunate she has her job, now that my dad's lost his."

"Still no luck?"

19

"No. I feel so sorry for him. He leaves the house about the same time we do, doesn't get home until five. How depressing it must be to spend all day looking for a job."

"I know. But consider the bright side. Because of people like your father, my mom's business is flourishing."

"Gruesome," she said. And so she thought. It was just so incredible that after her father had had his job with the Department of Energy for so many years, all of a sudden the government decided it didn't need a department of energy. And it didn't need people from a lot of other agencies, either. They were fired—only it wasn't called "fired" in Washington, D.C. It was termed "Reduction in Force." Or, in governmentese "RIF"; the verb, to be "RIFfed." Besides her father, it had happened to several other people they knew. What were these ex-employees to do? They still had to go on living, eating, buying clothes, gas, paying the mortgage. All financial concerns she'd rather not know about, as there didn't seem to be any solution for their money problems except waiting for Dad to get a job, for luck to strike.

It had struck Willy's mother. She was a psychologist who now spent her days trying to help people cope with what they had never been without before—a job. With the loss of employment there was not only a lack of money but also a loss of self-esteem, a loss of identity. At least that's what Willy's mother had said when she appeared on a radio talk show. Mrs. Nathan had also discussed the strain on one's marriage that the loss of income created. Kara didn't think that was why Mr. and Mrs. Nathan had broken up. Even Willy didn't exactly know why his parents had separated. Just one day they'd come to him and said that while they both loved him very much, they no longer loved each other. Therefore, they were getting a divorce. And Willy had turned to the Pretender.

That was the trouble with life, Kara philosophized. It was so impermanent. Jobs, marriages, love—nothing lasted forever.

"What kind of job is your father looking for?" Willy asked.

"I don't know. Same kind of job as he had before, I suppose."

"And he spends all day doing it?"

"Well, he's gone all day."

"Hm."

She put down her pen. "What does that mean, Willy?"

"I don't know. I just hear these stories from my mother. Like how her clients claim to be looking for work, but actually they go to a bar and drink the afternoon away."

"And you think my father would do something like that? You've got to be kidding. Anyway, I'd know if he even had a beer. No such smell at five o'clock. Besides, each night he comes home with a briefcase. A locked briefcase."

"A locked briefcase," Willy repeated. He thumped his pen on the table and thought it over. "Maybe he has found a job, then."

"He would have told us."

"Maybe it's something he can't tell you."

"And why not?"

"Like maybe he's a courier for a secret organization."

Kara sighed. "Willy, this isn't one of your books we're talking about. This is my father."

"Do you think none of the men in the Central Intelligence Agency has children?"

"Central Intelligence Agency? Oh, Willy, if he was RIFfed from the Department of Energy, they're not going to hire him at the CIA." Kara tried to return to her work but couldn't. She looked up again and confided in Willy. "I wish Dad would find a job so everything would be the way it was before."

"Yeah," Willy agreed somberly.

And then Kara was sorry she had said anything because, from the way Willy had said "Yeah," she knew he was thinking about his own parents and hoping that somehow they would get back together again so everything would be normal for him, too.

The stove alarm rang. Four thirty. "I'll get it!" Kara

called so her mother wouldn't come into the kitchen and complain about their smell again. She rose and opened the door to the refrigerator. Inside was a Corning Ware dish covered in foil. A white slip of paper rested on top. "Tonight," it read. She took the dish from the refrigerator, removed the paper, and stuffed the dish into the warming oven. Ever since he lost his job, Dad had taken up cooking, constructing daily casseroles for four, always for under five dollars—and boy, did they taste like it. But neither she nor Doug had the heart to tell him, mainly because he would probably suggest they make dinner themselves. Kara didn't see herself as a kitchen person. She had even chosen woodworking over home economics as an elective in school.

"Okay," Willy said as Kara sat down again, "which should it be? Leave good enough alone or leave well enough alone?"

Kara grieved. Decisions, decisions.

At ten after five the front door opened. "I'm home!" Mr. Valvano called.

"Hi, Dad. We're here in the kitchen," Kara said with enthusiasm.

She studied her father as he approached the kitchen. Okay, so he was old. Forty-two. But he was still handsome. A trifle thin perhaps—but what man wouldn't be after living for months on his own cooking?

"What smells in here?" he asked as he leaned down

to kiss his daughter.

"Oh, a wet dog," Willy responded. "We found it roaming around in the park and brought it up here to bandage its paw."

"Oh," Mr. Valvano said. He turned to walk away.

They didn't start giggling until he had reached the stairs and was going up them.

"You're right," Willy said. "He doesn't drink. I would have smelled it. But I doubt if he's CIA either."

"I could have told you that," Kara scoffed.

"His briefcase doesn't have a chain handcuffing it to his right hand."

"Maybe that's because he's left-handed," she countered.

Willy cleared out fifteen minutes before they were to eat, giving Kara time to set the table. She moved efficiently around her father as he made a last minute salad and put the rolls in the oven to brown. At five forty-five Kara went to the stairs and shouted, "Dinner!"

In the living room, her mother rose and put the paper down on the coffee table. It was her brother Kara was annoyed at. Doug was in his room with the door closed, listening to the radio. Sometimes she had to go upstairs and pound on the door before he heard her. But tonight his door opened like an explosion and he beat a tattoo down the stairs.

Kara loved this time, mealtime. From five forty-five

to half-past six they sat at the kitchen table together as a family, discussing the day's events.

"How's the training going?" her father asked her.

"Fine," she said.

"Why are you training in January when your first spring meet's not until April?" Doug was managing to feign interest and make fun of her at the same time, Kara thought. Brothers!

"Because the body needs to be kept in condition, something you should remember," she shot back at him. "By the way, my track shoes are falling apart."

A tight silence circled the table.

"I couldn't help it, really. Overuse," she diagnosed.

"I'll take you down to Shollecks' this weekend for a new pair," her father offered.

"This is the second pair of track shoes this school year," Mrs. Valvano noted quietly.

Kara glanced at her before returning her attention to the tuna casserole. Her mother's face was tight now, with lines that Kara had not seen before. Not the smile lines she was used to, but worry lines. "Well, I guess the shoes could last a few more months," Kara conceded.

"Nonsense," her father said with a smile. "A professional like you needs to dress the part."

"Well, if you're sure," Kara said.

"Of course we're sure," her mother confirmed. "Think of what would happen to your feet if your shoes fell apart on you during a race. We certainly can't buy you new feet."

"Yeah, if they go by size, they'd be very expensive," Doug said.

"Very funny," Kara replied.

"Well, you don't need new track shoes, do you, Doug?" his father asked.

"No-o-o." He drew the vowel out.

"But there is something you do need," his mother prodded.

"I just wanted to know if Dad would be available the night of January 23."

"I guess so, but why?" his father asked.

"Well, see, I—uh—I've invited Cindy Ballentine to the Snow Ball, and she's agreed to go with me. So I thought maybe if you would be willing to drive us—"

"Cindy Ballentine!" Kara shot at him.

"Yes."

"Going out with you?"

"What's wrong with Cindy Ballentine?" Mrs. Valvano inquired with concern.

"Cindy Ballentine, Miss Pompon." Kara was warming up.

"What is that supposed to mean?" her father asked. "Is Cindy Ballentine an older woman?"

"Well, if that's your type, Doug, go for it," Kara sneered.

"Not everyone goes out for cross-country and track," he chastised her.

"In this modern day not every girl spends the ball games shaking her pompons."

"Kara!" her father admonished.

"It's time for women to stop standing on the sidelines," Kara orated.

"She doesn't just stand." Doug defended Cindy. "She does cartwheels and splits."

Kara threw her napkin down in disgust. "Doesn't anyone here understand women's rights?" The table was silent.

"Your first date." Mrs. Valvano turned to her son with a bright young smile.

"I'll be happy to serve as your chauffeur," his father informed him with gravity.

4

As it turned out, Doug's father didn't have to serve as chauffeur after all. Cindy arranged for them to ride in Red Bucknell's 1968 Oldsmobile.

In a way Doug was just as uneasy with that situation as he would have been with his father driving. He didn't know anyone who would be in the car, except Cindy. Sure, he had heard about them. Red Bucknell and Bob Aioke were both on the varsity football team. Michelle Tourney, Cindy's friend, was a junior varsity cheerleader. And Ellen MacLean, Bob's date, was on the varsity swim team. He didn't know how a second trumpet would fit exactly with this type of crowd. But Cindy seemed pleased with the arrangement, so he guessed he should be too. After all, how hard would it be to spend just one night with them?

The Snow Ball was an occasion that called for a tie and a suit or sports coat. As usual, it was announced over the public address system that if anyone could not meet the required dress code because of financial need he could report to the office where confidential help would be given.

Doug had a suit jacket. His father's. He had a tie.

His father's. When he saw himself dressed up in them, he thought it might have been better to go in for confidential help.

"You look great," Mr. Valvano said to his son.

"Oh, yeah."

"You'll wow them."

"Are you sure it doesn't look like I'm playing dress-up?"

"To me it looks like you're playing dress-up because I remember you when you were wetting your diapers."

"Dad, please!" Doug said, his face reddening.

"But with objective eyes, sadly, you look like you're growing up. That doesn't mean that you'll no longer have need of your old father. Remember, if there's any trouble at all, you call me. I'll come and get you."

"There won't be any trouble, Dad."

"The dance ends at eleven?"

"Then we're going to Barbara Perrino's party." Another arrangement of Cindy's.

"One o'clock curfew then. Does that sound fair?"

"Yes. Anyway, Cindy has to be home by twelve thirty."

"Good."

Doug took one last look in the mirror, then got ready to race down the stairs.

"Do you need any money?"

Doug looked at his father, surprised at the offer, especially since he always got lectures about how he wasted his allowance buying record albums. "No. I already paid for the tickets, and I have a few dollars in my pocket for emergencies."

"Good. Remember, call if you need me. I'll be here all night."

"Yeah, yeah. I'll remember."

He ran down the stairs just as a horn started beeping in their driveway. Kara turned from the television in the living room to check him out. "Not bad," she complimented. "If you weren't my brother, I'd consider you an okay date."

Doug threw his parka over the suit jacket and gave her a smile. His mother rushed at him with the corsage for Cindy, which he had been keeping in the refrigerator. "No hanky panky," she warned him as she handed him the plastic box.

"Oh, Mother," he groaned, just as the horn in the driveway began to sound again. He dashed out the door, down the sidewalk, and into the back seat of Red Bucknell's Olds. He slammed the door and mumbled hello to Red, Michelle Tourney, Bob Aioke, and Ellen MacLean.

Michelle turned to the back seat and prattled on about how great the night was going to be while Red drove to Cindy's house, which sat on a corner lot, fenced in for her two Irish setters. He pulled into the driveway and began beeping his horn.

Wondering who had taught Red manners, Doug hurriedly got out of the car and rushed up to Cindy's door.

He rang the bell. It was opened swiftly by Mr. Ballentine. Doug caught sight of Cindy struggling to get into her dress coat without crushing the puffed sleeves of her gown.

"I expect you to take good care of her," Mr. Ballentine boomed at Doug before Doug even had a chance to introduce himself. "No drugs, no drinks, no—"

Hanky panky, Doug was sure he was about to say.

"Oh, Dad," Cindy chided him. She grabbed the corsage out of Doug's hands. "For me? Oh, thanks! It's great. See you later, folks." She grabbed Doug's arm and pulled him out the door.

"No later than twelve thirty," her father called after her.

"Don't pay any attention," Cindy said as they rushed to the car. "Dad does that to everyone."

Everyone? Doug was saddened by this revelation and the thought that he would have to live up to previous dates. But he had no time to get really sweaty palms about it because as soon as he and Cindy got into the car, Red took off, heading home to the playing fields of the Oakdale Wildcats.

When they arrived, the high-school parking lot was already three-quarters filled, and inside the school itself they had a hard time finding hangers for their coats in the makeshift cloakroom. Doug, being smaller than either Red or Bob, had no trouble snaking between them and retrieving two hangers. He fastidiously hung up Cindy's coat, then threw his parka over another bent wire and pushed open a space for both coats on the pipe rack.

Cindy was waiting for him as he came out of the press. She held the white corsage up to him, obviously expecting him to pin it onto her red dress. Taking the pin with the pearl drop on its end, he suddenly saw it as a lethal weapon. However was he going to attach the gardenias to Cindy's dress? If he did it without touching her, he would surely mar her shoulder. Then he would have to take her to the nurse. The most sensible way of securing the corsage was sticking his hand underneath her dress material. But—

Cindy watched him, her eyes laughing.

"You do it," he told her.

She took the pin and flowers from his hands and in one quick movement had the corsage perfectly placed and securely fastened. "It's just right, Doug," she told him, her voice soft, tender, romantically inclined. Nothing of the pom squad in it.

He took her hand and together they entered the gym, or what had been the gym before the decorations committee got at it and turned it into a winter palace of ice and snow.

Cindy rushed up to Megan, the chairman of the decorations committee, and lavishly extolled the committee's virtues. "It's nice," Doug told Megan when Cindy's words trailed into "Oohs."

"Thanks, Doug," Megan said with a wide smile. The two of them suffered through French class together.

The band started playing its first set. "May I?" Doug asked of Cindy.

"All the dances tonight are for you, Doug," she replied, in such a way that his heart sort of faltered. She came into his arms, and he thought he was living through a mirage. Cindy Ballentine, *the* Cindy Ballentine, being held by him, his gardenias pressed against their chests, the flowers alone standing between their heartbeats. Could any other guy be so lucky? He thought not.

Eleven o'clock and the band struck up a very poor imitation of "The Last Dance." The sparks from the first dance had not faded but had been showering continuously over Doug the whole evening. He hadn't known what to expect on this, his first date. He had dreamed, but the dream wasn't as sweet as the reality. He'd had hopes, and his hopes were more than fulfilled. What more could he ask from this perfect night? Except to be able to kiss Cindy good night? Without Red beeping his horn!

As he held Cindy tight for the last dance of the evening, Doug was shaken from his reverie by a short, fierce jab to his shoulder. "Hey! Let's go," Red Bucknell said with an eloquence entirely his own.

Doug had all but forgotten Barbara Perrino's after-the-dance party.

5

Mr. and Mrs. Perrino were standing by the front door of their house, waiting to greet the guests coming to their daughter's party. Trust between the generations was obviously lacking from the way their eyes darted over each newcomer. They reminded Doug a lot of his own parents.

Other partygoers pushed past the elder Perrinos in the entrance foyer as if Barbara's parents didn't exist, but Doug felt a compulsion to stop and introduce himself and Cindy. It was his training, what had been drummed into him since his first birthday party in nursery school. Introduce yourself. Shake hands. At the end of the party, tell the hostess what a wonderful time you've had. And don't wet your pants. That was when he was overexcited and didn't want to take time out to use the bathroom. Years ago. Years and years ago.

So Doug held out his hand to a nervous-looking Mr. Perrino. "Hi. I'm Doug Valvano, and this is Cindy Ballentine." Mr. Perrino seemed pleased to be going through the normal, civilized ritual of shaking hands. Doug looked at Cindy as they joined the throng. He hoped she didn't think of him as too much of a goody-goody.

"You're nice," she said to him sweetly.

They hit the buffet table and piled their plates high with cold cuts and chicken wings. Cindy held their plates while Doug went off into the kitchen. He came back with a bottle of 7-Up and two cups. Then they sat on the stairs, eating and talking about what a wonderful evening it had been, a wonderful dance, wonderful decorations. Doug wondered if Cindy could think him wonderful, too.

Some mustard smeared just above Cindy's lip. Doug wiped it off with his thumb, feeling the softness, the moistness of her. If only he could—but kissing her at the Perrinos' was out of the question. And kissing her in the back seat of Red Bucknell's car with Bob Aioke and Ellen MacLean looking on was not an appealing thought. On her front steps? Her father would be waiting for her.

"Hey, you guys!"

Mesmerized by the mustard staining his left thumb, Doug hadn't even noticed Michelle standing over them.

"Red wants to go. He says there's nothing to drink here, and you know how he is."

"There's plenty to drink. It's in the kitchen," Doug informed her.

Michelle just giggled. "L-i-q-u-o-r." She spelled it out for him.

Doug checked his watch. Eleven forty-five. Cindy had to be home by twelve thirty. "Let's let them go on," he said to Cindy. "It's almost your curfew. I'll call my father. He'll come over and pick us up in half an hour."

"Come on, guys, don't poop out on us," Michelle pleaded. "We're going to another party. Cindy." She drew her friend's name out several syllables' worth.

Cindy looked at Doug. "Well, if it gets too late at the other party, you could call your father from there."

Doug raised his shoulders. "Okay. It's your evening."

"You don't mind, do you, Doug?" she cajoled.

He smiled. "No. Not really." But he did. He couldn't see going off to another party with more people when all he really wanted right now was some time alone with Cindy. Maybe to embrace her, maybe to kiss her, if he dared. Yet how could he come right out and say that to her? So it was goodbye to this party and on to the next.

By the time Doug found his and Cindy's coats and said their thank-yous to Barbara and her parents, Red and the rest of them were in the car, and Red was leaning on his horn.

What would he do without it? Doug wondered. He slipped into the back seat beside Cindy, and Red took off so fast that the tires squealed. They drove out of densely populated Colesville onto the open road toward Ashton, past the horse farms, past the pastures, then through streets lined with 500,000-dollar homes. They bisected Ashton and turned toward the reservoir. Doug began to worry. Ashton kids went to their school, some of them. But who lived this far out?

In the middle of nowhere, Red Bucknell swung his Oldsmobile off the road into a field and parked it between a Toyota and a Datsun. As soon as he opened his car door, Doug could hear music from a stereo. Hard rock. Perhaps someone had rented a park pavilion. But that made no sense. All the parks were closed at dusk.

"This is the place!" Red said with growing excitement. Michelle laughed as he grabbed her hand and raced toward the music. Bob and Ellen followed.

"Well," Cindy said to Doug, "I guess we'd better go see what this is." It seemed to him that she was as uncertain, as unwilling, as he.

There was no pavilion. Just an open field where remnants of the Snow Ball had gathered.

Steven Mackey hustled up to them. "Five dollars a piece. Ten dollars a couple." He laughed wildly.

Doug reached for his wallet and removed ten dollars. He handed the money over to Steve.

"Okay, great. The stuff's over there."

Doug looked at Cindy, and was comforted to realize she didn't know just what "stuff" Steve referred to. Together they apprehensively made their way in the direction Steve had indicated. The stuff turned out to be liquor. Mostly beer, but also a few bottles of whiskey, a few of wine.

"Do you want anything?" Doug asked Cindy.

"Michelob," she replied, her voice subdued.

Doug grabbed two bottles of beer. Then they went over and joined a circle of kids. Most were from Oakdale, but a few were from other schools, judging from their jackets.

No one was talking much. This wasn't that sort of party. It seemed the object of this party was to drink, maybe even to get drunk, as fast as possible. Doug took a sip of the beer. It tasted sour in his mouth, as he was sure the dregs of the evening would, if this was the way it was going to end. Not that he had anything against liquor. Often his father and he had a beer together while watching the Redskins play on Sunday. But to sit and drink as if drinking were the only purpose in life didn't appeal to him.

Here and there a couple moved into the center of the circle and tried to dance. Joints made their way around the circle. Doug nursed his beer and watched while everyone pretended to be having a good time. Or maybe they were having a good time. Maybe he was the only one pretending. He glanced at Cindy. She would not turn to face him. Instead she was talking to Michelle. They would talk like lightning, and then a thunderstorm of giggles would follow.

Red Bucknell was on the other side of Michelle. He was drinking whiskey straight from the bottle. "Beer's too slow," he growled in a deep voice. Everyone laughed uproariously, everyone except Doug. He didn't especially like Red Bucknell in the first place and now, seeing him guzzle from a bottle like a skid-row bum, he was further unfavorably impressed. It occurred to him that he should have had his father drive after all. Maybe he would have dared a chance at kissing Cindy in the back seat while his father chauffeured. But now she wouldn't even look at him, as if they had done something to be ashamed of.

After a while Doug checked his watch. It was twelve thirty. He nudged Cindy and pressed the button that illuminated the dial for her.

"So?" she said.

"So. You're supposed to be home by twelve thirty."

"Oh, Daddy just says that. He doesn't mean it."

"He seemed to mean it to me."

"So what are we going to do, anyway?"

Good point.

"Get me another beer, will you, Doug?"

"Cindy, do you really want another beer?"

"Yeah. We paid for it. Anyway, what else is there to do here?"

He rose and made his way toward Steve's supplies. On his way, he passed by several couples making out in the dark. He brought Cindy back her beer. He uncapped it for her. She reached for it and took a swig. The beer ran down her chin and onto her party dress, shattering the image he had of her.

She laughed, she smiled, she shrugged. "Don't be such a pain," she told him. "Get with it."

He sat there and he thought. How should he get with it? It was past her curfew; soon it would be past his. They were out in the middle of nowhere; Red Bucknell was still chug-a-lugging the whiskey; and Cindy was barely speaking to him. Was this a moment to enjoy? He was bored to death.

One o'clock rolled by. His curfew. Fate had him in its grip. He couldn't shake loose. Unlike the others, maybe he didn't have the capacity to free himself. He was almost angry. Did he always have to be so under control while everyone else was getting high? High on drugs, high on liquor. They were high on the fact that they were high. He thought of Miss Lubovitch, his English teacher, and finally found something amusing in this fiasco. If she were here, she would throw a fit, listening to them. Conversations were composed of "You know?" The reply to which was, "Yeah, you know?"

One thirty. Anxiety was becoming terminal now. Doug hadn't said a word to anyone for the last twenty minutes. That didn't mean his mind was empty. It was full enough of what his father would say to him once he got home, and what Cindy's father would say to him.

How could he explain it? Well, we left Barbara Perrino's party and decided to drive to a field in Ashton and get drunk? Gee, you should have seen Red put it away? If his father ever found out he drove home with a drunk, he would—well, Doug didn't really know what he would do.

He remembered that time he had been in fifth, maybe sixth grade. His mother and father had gone out to see a movie, and they had allowed him to baby-sit for Kara. Only two hours, they would be back by nine thirty, they promised. But it had gotten later and later, and he had grown more and more worried, and still they did not come home. When they finally arrived, his mother's face was white, his father's hands were shaking. They had been in an accident. The driver of the car was a sixteen year old, coming around a curve at fifty miles an hour. There was no way he could control his car as it skidded. Doug's father at the last moment had veered off the road, trying to avoid him.

Both automobiles were totaled. The boy had a blood alcohol level of .2. He was almost dead drunk. Doug remembered all the concerned calls to the hospital his mother and father had made. Of course it wasn't their fault, but they still felt guilty and angry and bewildered. He wondered what his parents would say if they could see what was happening here?

They couldn't see, but someone else could. All of

the sudden, the secretiveness of their illegal gathering was shattered as headlights flooded the field, illuminating the group of them. "You kids get out of there or I'm going to call the cops! You can hear your noise from half a mile away."

A barrage of obscenities boomed over the field at the stopped truck.

"Okay," the man replied. "It takes me five minutes to get home from here. And it will take the cops five minutes to reach this place after I've called them. That gives you ten minutes to clear out."

He didn't wait for their reply, which followed him down the highway.

"Okay, come on," Steve Mackey yelled. "Someone help me load the liquor into my van. You want to party again next weekend, don't you?"

But Steve had overestimated their desire to party. It was every man for himself as the partygoers made a run for it. No one wanted to phone home from the police station.

6

Red Bucknell stumbled up the hill toward his car. Bob Aioke rushed after him and gave him support. Doug looked back to where Red had been sitting. The whiskey bottle was three-quarters empty. Had Red shared it with anyone? How much had he drunk himself? How much booze? How much pot? Could he still drive? What choice did Doug have?

"I'll be okay once I get to the car," Red insisted.

"You've really done it this time, partner," Bob said, laughing.

"Oh, Red, I'm just so upset with you," Michelle chided him, as if he were a child.

"Don't worry, baby. I'll have you home in a jiffy."

If he could find his keys. Doug watched while Red's fingers fumbled along the outline of his pants' pocket. It took him three attempts to hit the angled opening.

"Let's try to find another ride," he whispered to Cindy.

She turned on him with something akin to rage. "Don't be silly."

"He's drunk," Doug whispered.

"Well, so am I," she observed.

"Bob, why don't you drive?" Doug asked. "I think Red's had it."

"Hey! Nobody drives this Olds but me," Red informed him harshly.

The keys were in his hand now. He dropped them. Michelle picked them up and found the ignition key for him. They all piled in. To the right, to the left of them, cars were taking off in all directions.

"Time elapsed, four minutes," Ellen said, giggling.

"Don't worry. We'll be out of here before the cops can catch up with us."

Red started the car. Almost. He tried again. It roared into life. The car leaped foward. Then stalled.

"Reverse, dummy," Bob yelled with wild laughter.

Fortunately the Datsun and the Toyota were already gone, Doug thought.

Red reversed. All the way across the road into the field opposite.

"We're making progress," Bob encouraged him.

Red put the car into forward and finally succeeded in getting all four tires on the road at the same time. He stepped heavily on the gas and sped away from the reservoir.

"Take the back road home," Bob suggested. "We don't want the cops to pick us up going by Ashton."

"Right," Red agreed.

The Olds lurched. Doug saw the center line first to the left of the car, then to the right. At that moment, he knew if he stayed where he was he was going to die.

"Stop the car!" he shouted.

Red slammed on the brakes, and the Olds stopped dead center in the road.

Doug opened the back door. He got out and pulled Cindy after him. He went over to the front window which Red was rolling down. "Red, you are too drunk to drive. Let Bob try it."

"What do you mean by that?" Red snapped at him.

"Cindy, get back in here!" Michelle ordered.

Cindy tried to pull away from Doug. "No, she's not getting back in there," he told Michelle.

"This is my car. Who are you to tell me not to drive it? Either get back in now or I'm going. I mean it."

"Go, then. If it takes all night to walk home, at least we'll get there alive."

"You're crazy," Red said to him. "I always go to parties like this and I always bring 'em back alive. Don't I, Michelle?"

"You bet, honey. Get in here, you two," she pleaded. "Red's a perfectly safe driver no matter how much he's had to drink."

"Time elapsed, nine minutes," Ellen tolled.

Doug stood back and drew the protesting Cindy with him.

Red laughed and rolled his window back up. His horn honked and then he screeched off down the county highway.

7

Kara had fallen asleep listening to album rock on her clock radio. When the telephone rang, she thought it was part of the music, and she reached sleepily over to turn the radio off. She checked the dial of her clock. Two thirty. Who would be calling their house at two thirty at night? She planned on finding out.

When she went into the hallway, she was surprised to see the lights on downstairs. She slipped quietly to the head of the staircase and heard her father talking: "Yes, Mr. Ballentine. Yes, I am aware of the time. Believe me, I'm as anxious about them as you are."

Ballentine? Cindy's father? Did that mean that Doug hadn't come home yet? Oh, boy, was he in for it!

"I'll let you know if we hear anything. I'm terribly sorry. Yes. Goodbye."

"What did he say?" Kara heard her mother ask.

"Ballentine called the Bucknells. They have no idea where Red is, but they're not worried. I guess they're used to having him stay out all night."

"Oh, great."

"None of the other kids is home yet either. Ballentine called around."

"Well, if this Red stays out all night—"

"Yes. They could be anyplace."

"Why didn't Doug tell us there was a possibility of this happening?" her mother wondered angrily.

Because he didn't know, Kara wanted to march downstairs and inform her parents. This was his first real date, for heaven's sake, and Red's not his friend. None of them is his friend, except Cindy. I bet Doug is worried sick. I bet Doug is checking his watch every minute. I know Doug. He's so boringly responsible. It just wasn't fair for Dad and Mom to blame him. All kids do not live under the same rules.

Like take Willy. His mom didn't keep tabs on him. When Willy reached twelve years of age, he and his parents had had a conference and they told him that by his age he should know the difference between right and wrong and act on it. The responsibility for his actions was his own from then on. Willy had confessed to Kara that it was no fun doing outrageous things because his parents barely noticed. He reveled in hearing all the rules her parents set down for her and Doug, while she found them excessive.

"Do you think we should call the police?" she heard her mother ask in a cold, hollow voice.

"Oh, God, I don't know, Jan. They're probably out there riding around with that jerk, Red. He is their transportation, after all. What can Doug do about it?"

"There are so many things that could be happening."

"No. Doug's okay."

"I can't help remembering that accident we had. That boy was younger than Red Bucknell, and he was so drunk, he didn't even know he had been in an accident until after he had been in the hospital twenty-four hours. Do you remember, Tony?"

"Jan, stop thinking the worst."

"Something's wrong. I can feel it."

"Please, Jan! Stop being morbid."

Morbid. Kara squirmed. "Morbid." She knew how to use the word, but what did it mean? Exactly? French class: *Il est mort.* He is dead. Mom's got to be kidding if she's talking about Doug. Her brother, Doug. Doug, her older brother, her only brother.

Kara retreated to her bed. She really didn't know if she wanted to hear any more. Her mother was going off the deep end instead of thinking things through rationally. It was distressing to Kara. She resolutely turned over on her stomach. She had to try to get to sleep. When she woke up, everything would be okay. But her head had become a technicolor picture screen filled with terrible visions of what could be happening to Doug.

If he didn't get home safely, she would never forgive him. Never!

8

Cindy Ballentine watched open mouthed as Red Bucknell's car sped down the highway without them. When she turned on Doug, her voice was furious. "What did you do that for?"

"He was drunk." Doug thought it was self-explanatory.

"Do you realize what you've done? We're in the middle of nowhere. Nowhere!"

"Would you rather be riding around with Red as he tries to stay on the road?"

"Yes! Oh, what a fool I've been!" Cindy exclaimed, raising her fist toward heaven. "Michelle told me not to accept a date with you; she warned me. But oh, no, I had to get even with Charlie Sims by accepting the first person who asked me. And Red didn't even want to take you tonight. Michelle had to beg him. He said you were a wimp, and boy, was he right."

Doug just stood there as one shock wave after another buffeted him. Cindy, his Cindy, his perfect dream girl, was sounding off like a madwoman. "I—I thought you liked me," he said plaintively.

She looked at him. She must have seen that she had

hurt him because she changed tactics. "If you felt so strongly about not riding with Red, you could have at least left me in the car. How are we going to get home now? Do you realize what my parents are going to say?"

Doug checked his watch. Two thirty-five. It wasn't really Cindy's parents he was worried about. It was his. "Look, Cindy, you're my date. You're my responsibility."

"That attitude went out with the Dark Ages."

"Well, just pretend I'm still your knight in shining armor."

"Ha! After tonight I never want to see you again."

He didn't want to tell her that at the moment he was feeling the same way about her. "Red couldn't even stay on the road," he again attempted to explain. "I'm not about to sacrifice my life to be in with the in-crowd. Nor yours. On Monday you can tell everyone in school how wimpy I am, how awful your date was. I'm sure they'll all forgive you for my forcing you out of the great Red Bucknell's car. Right now let's worry about getting home. It just so happens I know where we are. My father used to take me fishing up at the reservoir. If we follow this road—"

"Follow it how?"

"We'll walk it. Come on." He took her hand. She pulled away, so he started walking without her. When she followed unwillingly in his footsteps, he slowed down to let her catch up. Soon she was hobbling along beside him.

Doug looked down at Cindy's feet. Her high-heeled black sandals were fine for dancing but not for walking along a blacktopped highway. He was torn. He knew he had to slow down for her sake, but he wanted to rush forward to reach safety.

The night was dark, the sky clouded over. The wind whipped against them. The only sounds were their own footsteps.

"It's cold," Cindy complained.

Doug watched as she tried to clutch her dress coat tighter to her. He knew what she was feeling. His mom had bought Kara a dress coat for special occasions. Kara had worn it once, to a concert at the Kennedy Center. "Is that thing supposed to keep me warm?" she had complained. "The wind goes right through it." He had smiled, but he guessed it was not funny for a girl, torn between wanting to look pretty and wanting to stay warm.

He took off his parka and held it open for Cindy to slip into.

"Don't be silly," she said to him, unnerved by his kindness.

"Come on. I have my suit jacket. It's just as warm as that coat you're wearing."

Cindy was wrenched between being grateful and holding onto her anger.

"We wouldn't be in this fix if you hadn't—"

"Yeah, yeah, I know," he said, helping her zip the parka up.

They walked. Doug checked his watch. Two forty now. Not a house in sight. Well, there wouldn't be. Not along this road.

"A car!" Cindy said before he even heard it.

"We'll flag it down."

"What if it's the cops?"

"They'll give us a ride."

She pulled him quickly off the road and into the woods. They ducked. A green police car swooped by them.

Doug looked at Cindy. "That was dumb."

"Oh, really? Well, if it's one thing I don't need tonight, it's to call my parents from a police station."

Doug considered it. "Yes," he agreed. "You're right."

"Besides, the police would only ask questions, like what are we doing out here this late at night? Like where were we? Who were we with?"

"Okay. You've made your point."

They got back on the road and walked. Minutes later a light glimmered in the distance.

"What's that?" Cindy asked hopefully.

"That should be the crossroads, the gas station."

"Will there be a phone?"

Doug looked at her and shrugged. "There'd better be."

The thought of help speeded them on their way. Even Cindy's shoes seemed to dance her forward. The lights grew brighter, the gas station became clearer. A phone booth stood at the corner of its lot.

"If only it hasn't been vandalized." Cindy sounded as if she were praying.

They rushed to it and pushed open the door of the booth. Doug picked up the phone. "A dial tone," he said with a gush of relief. "Oh, oh."

"What's wrong?" Cindy panicked.

"I don't have any money. I didn't bring change because it would jingle in my pocket, and I wanted to impress you."

She smiled and held up a purse no bigger than a baby's mitten. "My mother always makes me bring money along for emergency phone calls."

She dropped twenty cents into the slots.

"Your parents or mine?" Doug asked.

"Not mine," she begged.

Doug punched out the familiar number he had known since kindergarten. With fear and trembling in his heart, he heard the phone ring on the other end of the line.

9

His father answered before the first ring was completed. "Yes?"

"Dad!"

"Doug, where are you?"

"You know that gas station straight down the road from the reservoir where we used to go fishing?"

"The back road behind Ashton?"

"Yes."

"The one where we used to stop for Cokes?"

"Yeah."

"Yes. I know it. Where's Cindy?"

"She's with me."

"Is she all right?"

"Yes. We're both all right."

"I suppose you realize that we've been worried sick about you."

"Yes. Sorry. It's a long story, Dad."

"Stay where you are. I'll be right there."

"Hey, Dad!"

"Yes?"

"Cindy says can you call her parents."

"Yes. Right away."

Tony Valvano put down the phone. He looked at his wife. "They're over by the reservoir above Ashton."

"*Where?*"

"You call the Ballentines. I'm going after them." He threw open the door to the coat closet.

She rushed to him. "Tony, don't lose your temper in front of Cindy."

"And how do you expect me to hold it in? It's almost three thirty!"

"They're safe. That's all that's important right now."

"Just call the Ballentines."

"Right. Then I'm going upstairs and start counting my gray hairs."

He took his wife in his arms and gave her a quick, tight squeeze.

Kara, upstairs, still awake, felt relief rush through her. Doug had called. Doug was safe. Nothing morbid had happened. Thank God.

10

Now that rescue was near, Doug and Cindy became almost high with relief. "Oh, are we in for it," Cindy warned him. "Michelle's probably home tucked in her bed already. What's your father going to say?"

"Nothing in front of you. Mom will have warned him not to lose his temper. He'll be tight lipped and fatally grim."

She giggled. "My dad will be shouting. The moment he sees your father's car, he'll come storming out of the house like a raging bull."

"Oh, great. Will he give me a black eye or a swollen lip?"

"Neither. I'll stand between you. I promise. Do you realize he probably won't let me out for months? Oh, Doug, I will never forgive you for this date."

"Don't worry, after this evening I'll probably be so screwed up that I'll never ask a girl for a date again."

They were laughing when Mr. Valvano spotted them, laughing when their parents had been dying with fright.

He pulled up next to them, leaned over, and unlocked the passenger door. They struggled with each other over who would not get in first. Doug finally got up the courage to slip in beside his father, and Cindy huddled in next to him, managing to slam the door and lock it.

"Seat belts," Doug's father said.

Doug helped Cindy adjust hers. Then he said, "Dad, I don't think you've met Cindy Ballentine."

"Hello, Mr. Valvano," Cindy said in a very small voice.

"Hello, Cindy."

Doug wondered if a growl could sound like a hiss. Perhaps just before a volcano erupted.

At least his father didn't try to make conversation on the way home. Nobody did. They sat uncomfortably together, three to the front seat, and stared at the road.

When they reached Colesville, Cindy gave directions to her house. Mr. Valvano pulled into the driveway, stopped the car, and got out. Cindy slid out the passenger side; Doug followed. Rushing from the front door of Cindy's house came Mr. Ballentine, like a raging bull.

Cindy moved toward her father, who was practically pawing the ground.

"I'm terribly sorry about this," Mr. Valvano began. "I have not heard the explanation yet. I think we both should listen before we explode."

Mr. Ballentine jabbed his finger several times at Mr. Valvano and Doug without saying a word. Finally he got it out. "If I ever catch your son even sniffing around my daughter, I'll break his neck. Go on, Cindy. Get inside. Your mother wants a word with you."

He grabbed her by the arm. Cindy zipped off Doug's parka and escaped from her father long enough to return it to Doug. "Call you," she mouthed before she beat a hasty retreat up the front walkway.

Doug and his father returned to the car. Mr. Valvano pulled out of the driveway and headed toward home. "Words cannot express how I am feeling right now."

"No, sir. I mean, yes, sir," Doug tried.

"I don't think I was even this humiliated when I was called in and told I had lost my job. I might be wrong there, but I don't think so."

"Yes, sir. I mean, no, sir."

"You can cut the 'sir' business, Doug. It's not going to help," Mr. Valvano said as he pulled into the carport. Doug noted with despair that his mother was waiting by the open door. He went slowly up the path behind his father.

"Do you know how worried we've been!" she scolded him as he entered the house.

They marched him to the living room. "I want to hear it all," his father warned.

"All?"

"All," his mother agreed.

While Doug was deciding how to start, Kara crept down the stairs and sat on the bottom step.

"The trouble started—"

"Not the trouble, Doug," his mother warned. "Start at the beginning."

"We went to the dance. That was great. Then we went to Barbara Perrino's. I was having fun at Barbara's party, but Red wanted to go to another party. He wanted something to drink."

"Drink? Liquor?" his mother asked.

"Yes. I wanted to call you from Barbara's but Cindy said no, let's go on. So I figured I could call you from the next party. Honest. See, it wasn't even twelve at that point. But the next party wasn't at a house, it was at the reservoir. There were no phones. Obviously. There was only drinking and—"

"And!"

"There were a few joints passed around." Doug's voice was low. "Well, anyway, I mean, it was impossible to leave. Red was drinking a lot. I think. I didn't really watch him too closely. But then a man, some local guy, yelled from the road that he would call the cops if we didn't get out of there. So we got. Only— okay, see, Red couldn't even stay on the road. So I made him stop the car, and Cindy and I got out. You can guess the rest. We had to walk to the gas station. Then we called you."

"Cindy and you got out of the car?"

"Yes. She didn't want to. I made her. Red was swerving all over the road. I was afraid. Boy, was he drunk."

"You should have called from Barbara's," his mother Monday-morning quarterbacked.

"I realize that now, Mom, but not then. I thought the next party was at someone's house. How was I to know it would be in a field?"

"Well, you should have known what kind of person this Red was," his father insisted. "You should have told Cindy that I would drive."

"I hadn't heard anything about Red's drinking. All I knew about him was what everybody knew. He's the varsity football star. But I guess with the season over, he's no longer in training. And anyway, do you know how embarrassing it is to have your father drive you?"

"Is what happened tonight any less embarrassing?"

Doug thought that one over. His father had a point there, if only he knew. By Monday all the kids would hear about what a chicken he was, what a wimp. He would be the laughingstock of the whole school. And the stories Cindy would spread about him! Well, he really didn't blame her. It was obvious that she hadn't wanted to be his date in the first place. And now that she was in trouble at home, she would really want to get back at him.

"Well, in a way, you did the right thing," his mother conceded.

"You shouldn't have let yourself get caught in such a dumb situation," his father said.

"I don't know what we're going to do about this," his mother stated. "And I can't think straight tonight, after all the worry."

"Let's go to bed. We'll talk about punishments tomorrow," his father promised.

Just then, as if it were an alarm clock, the phone rang. Kara made a dash to the kitchen to get it. It was the first the rest of them knew she had been listening.

She came back toward the living room. "Doug, it's for you."

Doug looked at his parents, afraid they wouldn't let him take it. But they said nothing, so he rushed toward the phone. "Hello?"

"Doug, it's Cindy." Her voice was a whisper.

"Cindy? Are you all right? What did they do to you?"

"Dad's voice is gone so I'll be all right till tomorrow. Hey! Guess what just happened, though."

"What?"

"Mrs. Tourney called."

"Michelle's mother?"

"Yes. Michelle hasn't made it home yet."

Doug was surprised. Michelle had to have made it home before they did.

"Do you suppose they went on to another party?" Cindy asked.

"Yeah," Doug said. "Sure. That must be what happened. There's no way we could have made it home before she did."

"I know. That's what I thought, too. I'll call you tomorrow. If I can." She hung up.

"What was that all about?" his mother asked him.

"It was Cindy. Michelle isn't home yet. Her parents are calling around."

His mother looked at him, her anger renewed. "Kids!" she muttered, incensed.

11

Doug slept. He had no dreams. The cool air, the tiring night had taken them away from him. He slept knowing that the day he slept into was Sunday. There would be no disturbances unless a friend called and asked if he wanted to go to the movies. He knew what the answer to that would be already. There would be no movies for him, not after last night, not for a long while.

The phone rang like an alarm. Over and over it shuttled into his sleep. Someone would get it, his mind assured him, as he tried to bury himself deeper in his blankets.

Feet were scrambling in the hall. Small feet, light feet. Kara's. He heard her rush down the stairs and drop the phone as she grabbed for it. Opening his eyes, he looked at the clock. Five past seven. Who could it be at this hour? Cindy? He felt a stir of hope.

Kara was suddenly beside him. "It's Sam Rosen," she said. "He sounds funny."

"Funny?" Doug sat up. "What did he say?"

"He said he didn't know what to say."

"Was that all? Does he want to talk to me?"

"He didn't ask to. And when I told him I'd call you, he screamed 'What?'"

Doug was as perplexed as Kara seemed to be. But he made his way down the stairs and picked up the phone reluctantly. Sam probably wanted to know how things had gone between him and Cindy. Did he have the nerve to tell the truth? "Hello," he said.

"Doug!"

"Yes."

"Is it really you?"

"Hey, what are you on?"

"Mom!" he heard Sam yell. "Doug's alive!" Strange people, the Rosens.

"Sam, did you wake me up this early to find out if I'm alive?" Doug didn't know whether to be annoyed or amused.

"No." His friend sounded choked up. "I was calling to offer my condolences to your parents." Sam seemed to be sobbing. "Didn't you hear the news at seven?" he managed to ask.

"No. Listen, you wouldn't believe what happened to me last night. I—"

"You were in Red Bucknell's car?" Sam interrupted.

"Yes. That's—"

"He crashed."

"What!"

"They're dead, Doug. All of them—all except Red."

"*No!*" Doug shouted the word.

"Chris called me just before seven—he said to listen to the news. They didn't give the names. It's the next-of-kin cop-out. But Chris got it from Tom, whose mother works in emergency over at Suburban Hospital. Tom's mother said that everyone in the car was dead except the driver, a redheaded kid who's in a coma. He was airlifted by helicopter to the University Shock Trauma Unit in Baltimore. See, then I listened to the radio, and they said three were dead; but I knew there were six people in the car, so I thought the radio made a mistake. Is Cindy—"

"Cindy and I got out of the car."

"Then it must have been Michelle—"

"Bob and Ellen."

The silence hummed on the line between them.

"Doug," Sam finally said. "I'm glad you're alive."

"Me, too. Listen, Sam, if you hear anything else, call me, will you?"

"Will do. Meanwhile I'm going to let everyone know the good news. Hey, what would we do in trig without you?"

Doug put the phone back in its cradle. He was numb. He had heard Sam's words, but he hadn't really taken them in yet.

He went upstairs and stopped before his parents' open bedroom door. He saw them as two rag dolls lying under the covers. He hesitated. How did one approach one's parents in their own bedroom? When he had been a child, he had taken a running leap to join

65

them. Now he knew things about bedrooms that he hadn't known then, and he was embarrassed.

He knocked on their door. They stirred slightly. Perhaps they didn't want to come back to reality any more than he had.

"Mom. Dad," he tried softly.

His mother opened her eyes; his father sat up in bed. They stared at him.

What could he say? "That was Sam on the phone. Sam Rosen."

They looked at him as if he were an idiot.

"Something terrible's happened."

The way they continued staring at him made him feel as if he were invisible, as if they could neither see nor hear him. He panicked. "Mom. Dad!"

"What is it, Doug?" his father asked.

"Something terrible."

"What terrible?" his mother said sharply.

"Sam Rosen called."

They looked at each other. He knew that look. It was annoyance.

"There's been an accident."

His father jumped out of bed. "Outside?"

"No. Last night."

His father sat back down on the bed, looking rather the worse for wear.

"Red Bucknell," Doug finally got out. "His car crashed. They're all dead."

"What?" his mother almost shouted. That brought Kara running.

"I mean they're not all dead," Doug corrected himself. "Red's alive. He's in a coma. In Baltimore."

"Where did you hear this?" his father asked.

"From Sam. He heard it from Chris who heard it from Tom, whose mother is a nurse at Suburban."

"Turn on the radio, Tony," his mother ordered.

Mr. Valvano obeyed. He spun the dial until he came to the all-news station. They listened in silence while the world's tragedies passed by them. "Locally . . ." the announcer began.

Locally Red Bucknell's Oldsmobile had been traveling at a high rate of speed down Route 255. For no apparent reason, on a straightaway, it had veered across the road and sheared through a wooded area on the other side. The three passengers had been killed instantly.

The driver was thrown clear of the car and had been flown to the Baltimore trauma center, where he was reported in critical condition. The state's medical examiner had reported that the blood alcohol concentration of the driver was .22 percent, .13 needed to be declared legally intoxicated. The three passengers in the car were above the driving-while-impaired level.

"In sports . . ."

The voice faded as Mr. Valvano switched off the radio.

"How much did you have to drink?" his mother asked Doug in a low voice.

"He wasn't drunk," her husband told her sharply.

"I'd like to hear it from him."

"One beer. Cindy had two. I don't think she even finished her second one," he said, remembering how some had spilled down her chin.

"Why did you go with these people? Why did you *go* with them!" his mother raged.

"He's alive," his father shouted at her.

"Oh, dear God, just barely." She burst into tears. Tears! Doug had never seen his mother cry. Ever. Parents weren't supposed to cry. Parents were invincible. He stepped back into the hallway, shaken and faint.

12

Cindy could not face Michelle's parents. That's what it came down to. She could face the police. They had called her parents to say they wanted to speak with her some time tomorrow. She had nothing to hide. She wasn't gulity. Except of incredible stupidity.

She could face her own parents because she was alive, and the worst of their punishments would be nothing in comparison to what had happened to Michelle.

Oh, God. She just could not face Michelle's parents. Why did her mother insist that she accompany them on a visit to the Tourneys?

Her mother said that friends don't leave friends alone at a time like this. Yet what comfort could she be to the Tourneys when she would be standing in front of them, alive, while Michelle lay dead in the morgue. Oh, God! She kept repeating the supplication.

She wanted to go to sleep. She wanted to pretend this was all a dream and, when she awoke, she would call Michelle. They would laugh and giggle about last night, about everything. About Doug, the wimp—the wimp who had saved her life.

Michelle. It was funny how Mrs. Tourney had been so happy when her daughter started going out with Red Bucknell. She had taken down her own high-school yearbook and shown the girls pictures of herself when she was a cheerleader. She had been dating Michelle's father, who was captain of the football team. "What crazy times we had." Mrs. Tourney had sighed with pleasure. Crazy times. Like these?

What would she do without Michelle? Cindy mourned, for herself more than any other. Michelle had been her best friend since sixth grade. What would it be like to walk down the halls of the high school without her, not to meet her in the cafeteria line, not to have anyone to share her secrets with. Her life would be empty. No one could replace Michelle.

"Cindy!"

Her mother was calling from somewhere inside the house. Cindy had known since six this morning that Michelle was dead. At first she hadn't believed it. Then she'd cried. Now she tried to place a value on her friend's life. But a friend is someone you don't look at objectively. A friend is someone who's there for you. A friend is someone you do things for willingly. A friend is someone who'll give up playing second base in softball and take center field because second base is the only spot you want to play. Michelle had done that for her.

"Cindy!"

She was angry. Angry that Red Bucknell had sur-

70

vived. It was awful to say so. She shouldn't say it. Especially as he was in a coma and he needed all the prayers he could get to survive. So she wouldn't be awful and wish him dead. She just wouldn't think about him. But if he lived! A fury built up inside of her. Michelle was dead. Bob was dead. Ellen was dead. The loss, like a wave, covered her.

"Cindy?" Her mother was at the door. "What are you doing? Look at you sitting there with clenched fists. Who are you going to fight?"

"Red Bucknell," Cindy whispered.

Her mother sat down on the bed next to her and hugged her to her breast, rocking her back and forth. Trying to soothe her. Not succeeding. "You were supposed to be getting dressed," she chided her gently.

"What can I say to her parents?"

"I wanted you to come over with me to see Doug Valvano's parents."

"You're going to see Doug?"

"I think after last night we owe them a personal apology. He saved your life."

Cindy smiled and the tears came once again. "Yes. Yes, he did," she fervently agreed.

Kara did not understand her parents. Something horrendous had happened, and her mother was downstairs making pancakes as if this were any other Sunday. Doug had miraculously walked away from an all-consuming fire, and her mother was making pancakes.

Okay, not everything was normal. Doug had gone off the deep end a while ago. "What did I do? What did I do?" he was asking no one in particular, pacing their parents' bedroom, his arms wrapped around himself, shivering. "Why didn't I stop him?"

"Why didn't you stop who?" their father asked.

"Red. Why didn't I stop Red from driving! Why didn't I make them get out, Dad? I killed those kids!"

"Don't be ridiculous!"

"Dad, I knew he was drunk."

"They knew he was drunk, too."

"Oh, no. Not like I knew. Because they were so out of it themselves. But I knew he couldn't drive. I *knew* he was going to kill someone."

"It's an expression, he's going to kill someone. No one takes it literally," his father said.

"But he did! He killed not someone but all three of them. Why didn't I *do* something!"

"You did. You got out of the car. You got Cindy out of the car."

"I could have demanded that he not drive," Doug continued like a madman. "I could have fought him."

"Doug, he was a member of the football team, wasn't he?" His father was pointing out the obvious. Doug was five-foot-ten and weighed one-forty.

"But there must have been some way I could have convinced the others to leave the car."

"What way?"

Doug thought back, thought back to their laughter,

thought back to Cindy's anger. What way? What way, indeed. And yet, something gnawed at him. "I feel," he began, noting that his father waited for his every word, "dirty and guilty and sick with myself."

"Because you survived and they didn't?"

"Yes. Maybe."

Mr. Valvano sighed. "Would it be better to be dead?"

The doorbell rang. It tolled in Doug's heart like a death knell. From somewhere downstairs he could hear his sister opening the front door, but the rest was lost as his mind traveled at high velocity, only backward, to the night before.

Then Kara was in front of him. "It's Mrs. Ballentine," she whispered dramatically.

Doug looked at her without comprehension while his father quickly stood up. "Who?"

"Mrs. Ballentine. Cindy's mother," Kara repeated.

"What's she doing here?" Doug asked.

"She wants to see you. And Dad."

"And you told her I was here?" Doug was angry, but he could see that his anger puzzled Kara.

"Mom told her. She's down there talking with Mrs. Ballentine now."

"I can't face Cindy's mother."

"Doug," his father said.

"I can't, Dad. I just can't. I can't see anyone. Don't you understand?"

Gently his father took him by the arm and pulled him

73

upright. "I understand perfectly." He straightened Doug's hair with his fingers. "I don't blame you for not wanting to see anyone, but there are certain things in situations like this that must be faced. And seeing Cindy's mother is one of them. Now, come on. Your mother and I will be with you."

Reluctantly, Doug allowed his father to escort him down the stairs.

They found Mrs. Ballentine in the living room. She stood up when she saw them enter. She was perhaps an inch taller than Cindy, her hair short and blond, while Cindy's was long and brown. She smiled. She had Cindy's smile. Or Cindy had hers.

"Mr. Valvano, hello. I'm Kathy Ballentine." She held out her hand first to the father, then to the son. "I want to apologize for last night," she began.

"There's no need to apologize," Mr. Valvano assured her.

"Oh, yes, there is. My husband is horrified today by his outbursts of last night. But you see, there was no way for us to know what was happening with the kids. And we were worried. Terribly worried. As it turns out, we had every reason to be."

When no one spoke, she continued, "What I really came by for was to thank Doug for having the guts to get Cindy out of that car when he did. If he hadn't—"

She didn't have to say anything more. They all knew what would have happened if he hadn't.

"I wish I had saved them all," Doug said almost to himself.

"Yes, I wish that too," Mrs. Ballentine agreed. "But you didn't, and as a mother, I am selfishly grateful that it was Cindy you saved."

"How is Cindy?" Mrs. Valvano asked.

Kathy Ballentine raised her shoulders and let them fall. "Devastated. Michelle and she were like sisters. She said to tell you, Doug, that she's very sorry for what she said last night. I don't know what that was."

Doug smiled, remembering everything Cindy said last night only too well.

"She says she'll see you in school tomorrow, and she hopes you'll forgive her."

Doug said nothing. Mrs. Ballentine left, explaining that her family planned to visit the Tourneys.

The day passed. Doug couldn't believe that the hours came and went like any other day. Friends called. He told them over and over again exactly what had happened, as if the story itself were a magical incantation that would release him. It didn't.

Willy dropped by. He and Kara decided to go running, but only over the short course. They wanted Doug to join them, but he couldn't move.

A reporter phoned. Mrs. Valvano answered. "No, he doesn't want to speak to reporters. What ghouls!" she said as she slammed down the phone.

Doug retreated to his room. He felt claustrophobic, as if he could never escape. Night came. He slept. Morning would come. He would rise. His life would go on. Three others had ended.

13

Doug sat alone on the bus to Oakdale. It was the way he sprawled in his seat, his legs sticking out almost to the aisle, the way he turned his head rigidly to the window, that let people know he wanted to sit alone. Well, alone, no. What he didn't want was to have to talk to anyone about what had happened. Not that he couldn't overhear their conversations. The name Red was prominently featured, plus speculation on how the team would do next year.

When he got off the bus, he saw knots of girls gathered together. They were holding their books to their hearts and crying. Blubbering, his father would have called it. With no shame. Crying to be seen to be crying. He wished he could cry.

He walked down the school's narrow corridor toward his locker. Abruptly he noticed the floor had been waxed over the weekend. It didn't make sense to him. The students would only scuff it up again with their snow-packed boots, their dripping jackets. He saw a small crowd by his locker. He was pleased to note that one of the crowd was Sam Rosen. He was not as pleased that another was Steve Mackey.

"I want a word with you," Steve Mackey said with threatening immediacy.

Doug looked at him. Mackey was a senior. He guessed that's why Steve looked stronger than he, and bigger and tougher. But beneath Steve's anger there was a certain smell Doug had only read about before. It was fear.

"Would you get away from my locker?" Doug said quietly.

"I want to talk to you."

"I've got to get my books for first period class. So move."

Undecided, but surrounded now by more of Doug's friends, Steve moved aside. He watched while Doug opened his locker. "The cops are here."

"Here in school?"

"Yeah."

Doug shrugged.

"You know what that means, don't you?"

Doug turned to face him. "No. What does that mean?"

"They're going to be asking questions."

"About what?"

"About Saturday night. Your name is on the list."

"So?"

"So what are you going to tell them?"

"Whatever they ask, I imagine."

"Hey, I could get into a lot of trouble."

"Yes." Doug nodded. "I imagine you could."

"Look, you think I like providing liquor for these parties? But someone's got to do it, and I'm over eighteen. So I do it as a friend."

"And charge five dollars a person for it."

"For expenses. What are you going to tell the cops?"

"Who says they want to see me?"

"I saw your name on the list in the office. So?" Steve demanded.

Doug looked at him, disturbed, depressed, despairing. "Let me see your hands."

"My hands?"

"Your hands." Steve held them out. Doug looked at them. "I'm surprised. They're not red."

Steve whipped his hands behind him. "What does that mean?"

"Did you ever think, if you hadn't supplied liquor to Red—and to Bob and to Ellen, to all of us—that Michelle, Ellen, and Bob would still be alive?"

"What are you saying? It's not my fault if Red drank too much. After football season, he's always drunk on weekends. He should know his own limit by now. And if I didn't supply liquor for him, for all of you, someone else would. Remember that," he said as he backed away.

When he had almost departed from them, caught in the jet stream of traffic, Doug called out to him. "Hey, Steve, is your name on the list?"

"Yeah."

"What are *you* going to tell them?"

Steve gave him the finger and was lost forever.

"What a creep," Sam said. Chris and Tom nodded their agreement. Doug felt finally comforted, surrounded only by his friends.

"Welcome back to the land of the living," Tom remarked with a wide smile.

"I don't call this living," Doug answered. They laughed. He didn't know why they laughed. He hadn't said it to be funny.

"Did you see that write-up in the *Post*?" Chris asked Doug.

"No."

"Look for it when you get home. First page of the Metro section. Lots of sob-sister crap. There's an editorial, too. The *Post* thinks they should educate us to the dangers of alcohol, aside from raising the drinking age in the entire area so it's impossible to get it legally. What hypocrisy. As if drinking isn't the national pastime in Washington."

Doug really wasn't paying attention. Instead he asked Tom how Red was doing. "Did your mother hear anything?"

"Yes. The latest is that he's still in a coma, but he's responding to light and touch. Don't ask me how to interpret that."

"You mean if he comes out of his coma, he'll be okay?"

"It depends if you consider two broken legs okay."

"Two broken legs!" Sam repeated as if it were a circus trick.

"He gets off easy," Chris said. "Did you read what the *Post* said about the others? What happened to their bodies?"

Before he could tell them, the first bell for homeroom rang. The boys broke across the path of a passel of administration officials but caught a bit of what the men were talking about.

"All I'm asking is, does a moment of silence constitute prayer?" the assistant principal was saying. "Because prayer is out of the question."

"All right, what about calling it a memorial moment?" the principal substituted.

"It's just those parents out there. They hear we have prayer in the schools and they'll be down our throats. We don't need that *and* the police all in one day."

Sam looked at Doug and lifted his eyes. They split as Doug entered Mrs. Terrenova's homeroom and took his seat in the third row. The final bell rang, and Mrs. Terrenova began to call the roll, as a few stragglers dared to make their entrance without a slip from the office. Doug looked out the window facing the front of the school. He could see a single police car where the buses usually stood.

After attendance was taken, the P.A. opened up and blasted above them. The announcements followed. Spanish club, French club, science club, chess. Tryouts for the senior play, which this year would be *You Can't Take It With You.*

The announcements ended. There was the fumbling sound of the microphone being passed into other hands. "This is J. D. Heald, your principal, speaking," a man's voice boomed. "As I'm sure you all know by now, last Saturday night a tragedy overtook our little community here at Oakdale High. Three of our members were killed in tragic circumstances."

Doug sighed. Was there any other way to be killed?

"I know that they were well known to all of you. And as I read their names and their accomplishments, may we please have a memorial moment of silence to honor their young lives. Robert J. Aioke—halfback, varsity squad, Fighting Wildcats of Oakdale High School; third base, junior varsity baseball. Ellen Mac-Lean—varsity swim team, Spanish club, Future Nurses of America, junior thespians. Michelle Tourney—cheerleading, chorus, madrigals."

Mr. Heald's voice stopped. Doug watched the clock. The red second hand marched sixty steps before Mr. Heald's voice came back on. "There will be a discussion of this entire affair in your civics classes today. Have a good day, students."

The students' responding remarks to Mr. Heald were cut short by the bell ushering them toward first period. Doug was suddenly very glad there were bells, that he had a routine to follow, a routine to numb him toward the day ahead.

He wasn't called out of class until second period, just as Mr. DuBois was asking him to conjugate "avoir" in the future tense.

"Saved by the cops," someone muttered, as he left the classroom to follow the hall monitor. As he walked down the corridor, he spotted Cindy coming from the main office. She sighted him at the same moment and gave a short wave. "It was easy," she told him quickly as they passed. "They were very nice. They didn't even make you answer any questions you didn't want to. See you at lunch. Save me a seat."

She was gone without his saying a word.

When he got to the office, he was told to sit down. Miss Henry, the secretary, fixed him with her glare, and he already felt guilty. Of what he couldn't quite pinpoint. He shifted uneasily. He clasped his hands, he unclasped them. He put them on his knees, he folded them on his lap, he put them on the couch. Miss Henry zapped him with her eyes again. Stop fidgeting! her gaze said. He tried. Honestly.

His stomach dropped. He knew he was going to be sick. He wondered if it would be possible to ask for a pass to the nurse. He looked at Miss Henry again. No, he guessed it wouldn't.

Ten minutes of waiting. It seemed like a hundred. The door to the office finally opened. Out came Steve Mackey with his parents. Steve had been crying though he tried to hide it behind his hands. Steve saw him sitting there, waiting to see the police, and in a way Doug was glad. He didn't like Steve or respect him. He didn't plan to have anything further to do with him. But he also didn't want Steve to think that he had ratted on him. He didn't want anyone to think that.

Mr. Heald came out of the principal's office. Miss Henry handed him a slip of paper. He looked down at it, then up at Doug. "Doug Valvano?"

Doug stood. "Yes, sir." Mr. Heald didn't know him from Adam. Doug walked toward the door and saw two state policemen waiting inside the office. He entered.

They apprised him of his rights. He guessed that's what it could be called. They told him he didn't have to answer any of their questions. That if he wanted to, he could call his parents and/or his attorney. That at any time if he wanted to stop answering questions, he could. Then, with their questions, they returned him to that night, asking mainly about Red Bucknell. He told them. He told them how Red had been fine up until the time he drove to the party in the field. "I didn't know anything about that party. I thought we were going to someone else's house."

"Red said he wanted to get something to drink?"

"Yes. Well, no. Michelle came over and told us Red wanted to get something to drink."

"Can you swear to how much he drank at the field?"

"Swear to it? No. I knew he had a bottle of whiskey that was only a fourth full by the time we left the party.

1 don't know how much of it he drank. But he was drunk."

"Why do you say that?"

Doug grimaced. "You would say that if you had seen him. He couldn't walk. Like Bob had to help him up the hill to his car. I wanted to find another ride or get Bob to drive or something. But Red said he would be okay once he got in the car."

"Was he?"

"No. He—it was awful. He didn't know the difference between drive and reverse. And then when he finally got us on the road, we were all over it."

"How do you mean?"

"Swerving back and forth across it."

"And you told him to stop the car?"

"I was afraid. I was really scared. I had never been in a car with anyone driving like that. This was—it was my first date." He blushed. "It'll probably be my last."

"It could have been," the policeman said grimly. "Are you willing to sign a statement to this effect? To testify to this matter in a court of law?"

"Would I have to?"

"Yes, if there are court proceedings."

"What court proceedings?"

"Possible prosecution."

"Of Red?"

The policeman said nothing.

"But Red's in the hospital."

"And three other people are in the morgue. Did you know that Red Bucknell had a prior conviction for drunk driving?"

Doug was shaken. "No."

The policeman sighed. "Thank you, Doug. We'll definitely be in touch with you again."

Doug stood, startled and drained. There was to be, he suddenly realized, no end to this.

14

Cindy sat down across from Doug at the lunch table. He felt all eyes staring at him. Their sitting together was unusual. They were breaking with custom, which demanded that boys sit with boys, girls with girls. That was to discuss the morning's social events, like who had spoken to whom in the hallways, which couple might be breaking up, where next weekend's party would be held.

Cindy had an apple, a half pint of chocolate milk, and a bag of Fritos. "Hi," she said almost gaily. "What are you eating?"

He looked up at her, puzzled. She was acting as if nothing had happened, more specifically as if nothing had happened to them. She was waiting. "Bologna and cheese on rye," he told her.

"What kind of cheese?"

What kind of cheese! What did it matter? "American."

"White or—"

"Yellow."

She crunched into her apple. She smiled at him behind her first bite.

"Cindy . . ." he tried hesitantly to begin.

"Yes?"

"Don't you—do you feel anything?"

She looked at him as if he were a halfwit. Then she burst out crying. The tears just erupted from her eyes as if from a cloud breaking. Even as she cried, she turned red, obviously embarrassed that anyone should see her overcome by her emotions. Overcome in school.

Doug didn't know what to do. He didn't know whether to hold her or to run. In the end he simply gave her the yellow napkin he had packed with his lunch.

"Thanks," she told him, stifling her sobs. "I feel like such a jerk."

"No."

"Listen, don't pay any attention to what Michelle's mother says in the paper."

The paper again. What was in that article?

"I mean, she didn't know what she was doing, what she was saying. I know that for a fact. I was forced to visit her house yesterday. It was awful. What was I supposed to say? What was I supposed to do? Her parents were there. Her relatives. Some parents of other friends of hers. I felt I was the only one alive. Everyone was angry, but no one knew what to do."

Cindy stopped talking as abruptly as she had

started. Doug was still at a loss. He watched while her eyes dried up and narrowed into slits. "I hate Mr. Heald," she began again. "Simply hate him. What good did he think he was doing, reading their *accomplishments*. They accomplished nothing except to die young."

"Cindy—"

"No. It's true. I can just hear my epitaph: Cindy Ballentine, Pom Squad, 2."

"Cindy. It's not going to help."

"How do we choose what's important to us? Do you know I spent a whole summer learning the pom squad routines? Why? How could I have been so stupid!"

"It's not stupid to want what everyone else wants."

"You wouldn't know because you never wanted stupid things," she said.

"I wanted that date with you!" It just came out. He was shocked and aghast, but there it was on the table between them.

Cindy's mouth dropped open. And then she laughed. Wild laughter, modulating to real as Doug joined in.

"I am so dumb," she said with utter sincerity.

"No, you're not."

"Dumb. Dumb. Stupid. Ridiculously dumb. I was so blinded by the glory of the company I was in that I would have gladly ridden to my death. You saved me."

Doug made no reply.

"You saved my life," she assured him, looking earnestly into his eyes.

"I wish I had done more," he said, his eyes lowering away from hers.

She put her hand out across the table and let it rest on his, oblivious to the stares they were receiving. "I suppose you'll always wish that. I'm lucky in that respect. I know absolutely there was nothing I could have done to save any of them. That comes from being dumb. A lack of responsibility for my own actions."

"What do you think I should have done?" he asked her urgently.

She sat back. "You know what I think we both should have done, what I think about over and over again? We should have called your father from Barbara's party."

"But we didn't."

"I know. I hate myself for that, because that was my decision. If we had stayed at Barbara's, we wouldn't have had anything to do with this awful nightmare. Except to mourn."

"But we didn't," Doug repeated.

The conversation collapsed. They were both caught up in their own private circles of "if onlys."

Doug sat in Contemporary Issues civics class checking his homework assignments so far. Nothing too bad. In English, right before lunch, Miss Lubovitch had raved on about the glories of Samuel Johnson and James Boswell. Had they but known—it was all preparatory to a semester-long assignment. Buy a steno pad. Keep a diary of your own. Write in it every day and have it ready to turn in by semester break. "Dear Diary." The girls all *oohed* in expectation. Keep a diary. What was he supposed to say?

Mr. Valdez, the civics teacher, sprang into the classroom. "The Wetback," they called him when he wasn't around, good civics students that they were. Usually he discussed such fascinating subjects as reapportionment. Usually he had them composing meaningless letters to their governmental representatives. But today he plunged with gusto into the latest of current affairs. What would you do? There is a party in a field. Everyone is drinking, some more than others. You discover that your ride is drunk. You don't know how drunk until you get into the car and see he can't stay on the road. Having set up the situation, Mr. Valdez took a poll.

Three-fourths of the girls said they would have stayed in the car because they had to rely on their dates to bring them home. Though one of the girls added nastily that she wouldn't get into a car with anyone like Red Bucknell in the first place.

Half the boys said they would not have gotten out of the car. "It's chicken to get out," was the consensus. Doug looked at the ones who said this. They were jocks, they were student reps, they were popular. He noted the other half of the male contingent, the half who said they would have gotten out of the car. They were wimps like himself. He sighed. He barely listened to Mr. Valdez' talk about peer pressure. It occurred to him that not even death would have improved his standing among his fellows at Oakdale.

Mr. Valdez gauged his time. For the last ten minutes of the period, he gave a lecture on drinking and driving. The class listened but not too attentively. They had heard all this before. From teachers, from parents, from television, from police. "It's the breaks of the game," one fellow told Mr. Valdez as the bell rang. "You do your drinking and you take your chances."

"But you're taking your chances with someone else's life," Mr. Valdez reminded him.

It made little impression. Half the class was already out the door, craning to see who was meeting whom.

15

Cindy watched as the minute hand clicked into place. Three o'clock. The bell rang and school was over.

Three o'clock. Her favorite time of the day. That's when the action started. Usually. But not today.

Pom squad rehearsal was held at three-oh-five in the gym. She was supposed to be there. She had to be there. If she missed more than two rehearsals a semester, she would be kicked off the squad. But how could she go today when everything seemed so disjointed?

"Cindy, you coming?" Suzie Evans called.

"In a minute," Cindy answered, fumbling in her locker, pretending she was trying to find something.

She wanted to be alone. That was a little difficult in a school of twelve hundred students at a few minutes after three with everyone milling around the halls.

"Go on with your life," her mother had said when Cindy asked what she should do, how she should act.

Her life. Sugar and spice and everything nice. Until this weekend.

She grabbed her saddle shoes from the bottom of her

locker, then slammed the door with too much force. The locker door flew open at her and almost hit her in the face. It would have been a minor tragedy, she consoled herself. She closed the door more carefully, snapped her lock shut, and twisted the dial. Then she walked off toward the gym.

"Hey, Cindy!"

She turned to see Charlie Sims swaggering toward her. He wore his football jacket and his crooked smile. "Cindy, I just don't know what to say," he told her solemnly.

She shrugged. "There's nothing much that you can say."

"What an incredible—" He looked around the hall, as if searching for the right word on the cinderblocks.

"Yes," she agreed. "It was incredible."

"Bob. He was so—nice, you know?"

"Yeah." She smiled. "He was nice."

"Like I didn't get to know him real well because he didn't pal around with the rest of us too much. Did you know that he played the violin?"

"No."

"Yeah. His mom wouldn't let him play football unless he did something cultural. That's why he and Ellen dated. See, she played the flute and they belonged to some group together."

Cindy's eyes filled with tears which she did not wipe away.

"Cindy, I'm sorry. I didn't mean to make you cry."

94

"Oh, Charlie, I can't stop crying. It's just such a—a waste. Stupid," she muttered under her breath.

"Yeah," he agreed. "You're lucky you got out."

"It wasn't luck, Charlie. Doug Valvano got me out. He pulled me from the car."

"I heard."

"I would have stayed in the car," she said, as she had over and over before this. "What would you have done?" she wondered.

He shrugged and smiled. "I would have stayed in the car, too."

Cindy looked at Charlie and suddenly realized that if she had waited for him to ask her to the Snow Ball, she would be dead right now.

No, that's wasn't fair, she corrected herself. Charlie had access to his own car. And he didn't drink the way Red did. He'd have a few beers when they went out together, but he was never noticeably drunk. Her heart chilled then, because she remembered her civics teacher telling the class that with most drunk drivers you couldn't tell they were drunk from outward appearances. They could act normally, control themselves physically, then get in a car, drive off, and kill someone.

But not Charlie, she argued with herself. He never had that much to drink. "I can't think about it any more," she said, out loud but to herself, as she shook her head to clear it.

"Yeah, it wipes me out," Charlie agreed. "What did

your parents have to say to you about all this?"

"You just don't want to know."

"I guess that means you and I won't be able to go out this weekend."

"I may never get out of the house again," Cindy informed him with a touch of humor. "Anyway, I'm not ready to go out," she said more seriously. "It might take a long time to be ready to go out again."

"Well, look, I'll see you around though?"

"Sure, Charlie, we'll see each other."

He gave her a half salute and sort of backed away from her. She noticed the time and, with reflex born of habit, rushed toward the gym.

Miss Pritcher—just about everyone but the teachers called her Miss Bitcher—was putting the other eleven pom squad members through their paces. A vacant hole third from the right was waiting for Cindy. She wondered suddenly if the same thing was happening with the cheerleading squad, or if one of the alternates had already been selected to fill Michelle's place.

Miss Pritcher looked meaningfully up at the clock. Cindy dropped her books, took the last two pompons from what had been a pile, and hurried into line.

They were in the middle of their warm-up, which was always done to the Wildcats' fight song. It was so routine to Cindy that she didn't even think as she flailed her arms to the left, the right, up and down. She had a picture in her mind. It was of one temperate Saturday afternoon in October. The pom squad was out in front of the crowd doing their halftime routine to "Hey, Look Me Over." They were accompanied by the band. She smiled without realizing it. That was the first time she had really noticed Doug Valvano enough to be interested in him. Hey-look-her-over was exactly what he was trying to do. Which was pretty hard, considering he was playing his trumpet. First his trumpet was on one side of him and then it was the other. She'd thought it rather weird until it occurred to her that he was playing in that mad fashion only so he could get a better glimpse of her.

"Ballentine! Get on the *ball!*" Miss Pritcher boomed.

Cindy, lost in her thoughts, had fallen a few beats behind the rest of the squad. She looked around to find her place. A few seconds later the fight song ended. They were supposedly warmed up.

The girls waited until Miss Pritcher chose the routine she wanted them to practice next. They had fourteen days until School Spirit Week, a week devoted to making Oakdale students feel like a community. The pom squad's part in it was the pep rally, when they would join the cheerleaders in egging that community on.

Miss Pritcher picked the cassette she wanted. It was the "Semper Fidelis" march. Just what Cindy needed. She had to get her knees practically up to her chest with every step and swing her arms wildly.

Miss Pritcher watched them critically as they

pranced around the gym. She yelled so that her voice would be heard above the screeching tape. Names were called out as she corrected each tiny fault. More particularly Cindy's name, as it seemed that today she could do nothing right. "Put some life into it, Ballentine," Miss Pritcher raged.

She suddenly snapped the cassette off, leaving the girls in awkward positions as if they were playing statues. "This is disgusting!" she snarled at them. "How many weeks have we had to go over this, and you still are making mistakes. Don't think I'm not going to remember your attitudes when I pick the pom squad for next year," she threatened.

Lose the prestige of being on the pom squad? The thought horrified them, and the girls were suitably quelled. Except for Cindy, who suddenly saw the whole thing as being terribly ridiculous. "Is it really so important that we do everything perfectly?" she had the nerve to ask.

Shocked at this challenge to her authority, Miss Pritcher reacted with force. "Well, if you don't think it's important, Cindy Ballentine, perhaps you'd better leave."

None of the girls let out or took in a breath while Cindy calmly removed the pompons from her hands, placed them carefully where the pile would be, picked up her books, and walked out of the gym.

As she broke through the doors, Cindy felt suddenly free. Of what, she did not know.

16

Kara slammed into the house after her run with Willy. It had been an aggravating practice because, instead of picking up the pace as they were supposed to do, Willy kept asking questions about the accident, suggesting that maybe it was tied to her father's occupation.

When she tried to point out that her father didn't have an occupation any more, Willy blithely ignored her and theorized that someone was out to get her father through his family. Willy was obviously insane.

Still his insanity did bring into her mind questions that she should be asking, if not of her father, then of her mother. Mom would surely know what Dad was doing with his time. Kara would ask her and then face Willy with the true story so he could put his wild fantasies to rest.

"Mom!" Kara stood at the entrance to the living room and waited for her mother to acknowledge her presence. But her mother was staring at Doug, who was reading the paper.

It looked as if it might turn out to be a long wait. "Mom?"

Mrs. Valvano turned her head slowly toward her daughter. "Not now, Kara."

"When, then?"

"Later."

Later. Always later when she had something important to say. She rushed upstairs. She would do some homework while she waited for her mother to have time for her. Willy's theories were something she had to discuss with someone. She needed another person to reaffirm her view that this whole thing about her father and the CIA had come straight from Willy's unnervingly vivid imagination. She supposed that was one of the problems of reading all the time, as Willy did when he wasn't out running. It overstimulated the mind.

Mrs. Valvano could hear her daughter clomping around upstairs like a filly caught in its stall. Her heart burned for her, but it broke for Doug.

As soon as Doug had come in the door, he had wanted to see the paper. She'd hidden it from him this morning, but now he demanded it. So she turned it over to him and watched him read, mouthing each word as she always told him not to do.

Doug read the story headlined "Three Silver Spring Teenagers Killed in Crash." Three yearbook pictures and a shot of Red's Oldsmobile framed the words. It was odd because the car didn't really look too badly damaged. But the article pointed out that no one had been wearing seat belts. Michelle's head had crashed through the front windshield and her body had followed. Bob and Ellen, thrown over the back seat into the dashboard, had gone back and forth like yo-yos as the car settled against the tree.

The officer estimated the rate of speed to have been seventy miles per hour along a road posted at forty. There was no sign of the brakes having been applied. There was no sign that anyone knew what was going to happen. Doug thought about that. He would have known. He would have seen death approaching. If. If he still had been in the car.

Their lives were short and sweet, the reporter had discovered. Outstanding students. Popular with their classmates. Beloved of their families. The meaninglessness of it. The horror of it.

Michelle Tourney's mother was interviewed. Doug flipped to an inside page. Yes. There was a photograph of Mrs. Tourney holding a picture of Michelle and Cindy, their arms around each other. The reporter wrote about the two who were not in the car, how fate had separated these best friends, Cindy and Michelle, in the moments before death. "Why?" Michelle's mother asked. "Why, if this boy pulled Cindy out of the car, couldn't he have pulled Michelle out, too? Was she any less worth saving?"

Doug would not let the question touch his heart. Not

yet. He read on. Red Bucknell's father was interviewed, his mother being in constant attendance at the trauma center in Baltimore. "Red's an all-American boy," his father said. "The sort of son every father wishes for. He has a great future ahead of him. Yes. I knew he got drunk occasionally, but that's what all teenagers do. Think back to your own teenage years. What was life without somehow figuring out how to get a six-pack for Friday night? Poor Red. He just got caught. Now I'll have to see about getting him a new car to surprise him when he comes home from the hospital. There's nothing I wouldn't do for that boy."

Doug put the paper down. The article made it obvious even to him. Red was the hero. He himself was the villain. He could have saved them all, but he hadn't. While Red—there was no fault attached to Red. He was just doing what comes naturally to red-blooded Americans. He was driving drunk.

Doug rose and walked slowly to his room. His mother called after him, but he didn't hear her voice.

17

Doug was in the kitchen spreading mustard on two slices of rye bread for tomorrow's sandwich when he heard the doorbell ring, then ring again. He knew his parents were somewhere in the house, exactly where, he could not pinpoint. His father was probably down in his basement workshop, his mother maybe upstairs. Had either of them heard the bell?

As he started slowly to the front door, he saw his mother coming from upstairs. It was she who opened it to Willy and Kara and Willy's mother. "Oh, hi, Miriam," she said. "Thanks a lot for taking Kara to get those running shoes. Somehow it just got lost in the shuffle—this weekend."

"That's okay, Jan," Mrs. Nathan replied. "I managed to get a week's grocery shopping done while they decided on which pair to buy."

"The treads are important," Willy said.

"The arch support, too," Kara added.

"Hi, Doug." Mrs. Nathan had obviously had enough of running shoes for one evening.

"Hello, Mrs. Nathan. How are you?"

"I'm fine. More importantly, how are you?" She watched while, in reaction to her question, Doug simply shrugged. "I'm just down the street, if you should need me. I wanted you to know that."

"Thanks, Miriam, but I think he's hanging in there," Mrs. Valvano said.

"Fingernails grasping the edge?" she questioned him.

Doug smiled. "Just about."

"I realize you know me only as Willy's mother, but helping people is my business."

"Yes, Willy's been telling us how well you're doing," Mrs. Valvano said, almost defensively.

Mrs. Nathan laughed. "I'm not here drumming up business. I meant it as one friend to another."

"Sorry," Mrs. Valvano apologized. "It's been so—"

"Awful. Yes, I know. For all of you, I imagine. Well, I just wanted to let you know I cared. Willy, are you coming?"

"Can I stick around a while? Kara and I have some training procedures to discuss."

"I see. You don't want to help unload the groceries."

"Well—"

"See you at home, then. Not too late."

Doug retreated into the kitchen as soon as Mrs. Nathan left. He had expected to be alone, to finish his sandwich making, then to escape to his room in peace.

He had not counted on Willy and Kara's following him kitchenward, though, with their appetites, he well might have.

"Doug, can we talk to you for a second?" Willy asked.

"Not if it's about the accident," Doug warned.

"It's about Dad," Kara said.

"What about him?"

"Do you know what he's doing during the day?"

"Looking for a job, I suppose."

"That's what I told Willy."

"Well, then?"

"Why does your father carry around a locked briefcase?"

Doug looked at Willy, a trifle annoyed, a trifle amused. "Darned if I know."

"Willy thinks Dad's in the CIA. He's almost got me believing it!"

Doug plunged the knife into the mustard jar. "How did you come to that conclusion?"

"I finally asked Mom what Dad does during the day. She wouldn't tell me," Kara said. "She sort of put me off."

"That's a departure," Willy assessed.

"Departure from what?" Doug asked.

"Well, they're usually not allowed even to tell their wives, and yet it seems your mother has an inkling."

"Honestly, Willy!"

"It's just that she knows something that she's not telling us, Doug."

"Well, that's her right, isn't it?"

"If he's CIA and in danger, don't you think we ought to know?"

"Are you two getting enough oxygen, out there running all the time?"

"You're not taking us seriously, are you, Doug?" Willy demanded.

"No, I guess I'm not, Willy."

"It's always the least likely," Willy said grimly.

"Let me put it simply," Doug retorted. "You guys are crazy."

"It's Willy's idea, not mine," Kara stressed.

"What's in his briefcase? That's what I want to know," Willy said.

"Well, it's going to be a little hard to find out," Doug answered. "He always keeps it locked."

"Why though?" Kara asked.

"Because he doesn't want us to know what's in it." Doug thought the answer obvious.

"But why doesn't he want you to know what's in it?" Willy pondered.

Before Doug could be caught up in the spirit of their suggestions, the phone rang.

"I'm not answering it," Kara said. "I'm tired of being a messenger service."

Doug walked across the kitchen and picked up the

phone. It was for his father. He hurried past Kara and Willy to the basement entrance. "Hey, Dad! Phone's for you!"

"I'm coming."

All three watched while Mr. Valvano left the basement unguarded to answer the phone.

"Now's the time," Willy whispered.

"Time for what?" Kara asked.

"To see what's in the briefcase." Willy leaped up and made his way to the basement door. He motioned Kara to follow.

Kara tiptoed to the doorway while Doug watched. "We'd better not," she said.

"Don't you want to *know*?" Willy challenged.

"Isn't this a little bit insane?" Doug couldn't believe them.

"You don't have to come with us," Willy informed him generously. "Just keep watch."

"Please, Doug," Kara begged. "Willy's driving me crazy with this Pretender business. I've got to know."

Before Doug could object, they were gone, down the stairs. He could see them moving like mice along the wall.

Now what was he supposed to do? His father was still on the phone, Kara and Willy were in the basement, and he was stuck incriminatingly by the cellar door.

Darn! His father had hung up. He was coming down

the hallway toward Doug. Too bad Willy, who was so good at making things up, hadn't made up a code word of warning. "Hi, Dad!" Doug said loudly as his father approached.

"Hi, Doug." Mr. Valvano looked mystified, as if wondering if Doug thought he was hard of hearing. "Did you want to speak to me?"

"No." Doug grimaced nervously.

His father went past him and took two steps down the basement stairs.

"Dad!"

Mr. Valvano turned to face his son. "Yes, Doug?"

"Are you going back down into the basement?"

His father considered that for a minute. "Yes, Doug, I think I am."

"Well"—Doug waved—"have a nice time." Feeling like an idiot, he fled upstairs. Fifteen minutes later Kara was knocking on his door fiercely, demanding entrance.

"Why didn't you give us more warning?" Kara scolded, as she closed his door tightly behind her.

"What was I supposed to say: 'Hey, Kara and Willy, get away from the briefcase because Dad's coming'?"

"Well, he almost caught us. Luckily Willy pulled me out of Dad's study just in time."

"What did you tell him you were doing down there?"

"Learning how to use the washing machine."

108

Doug shook his head and returned to what he was doing.

"Don't you even want to know what we found?" she asked him.

"Dad's CIA decoder kit?"

His derision could not affect her. "His briefcase was full of computer cards. And on his desk was a green-and-white computer printout."

Doug looked up, finally interested.

"Willy thinks they have to do with the Russian gas fields."

"Why does Willy think that?"

"Because Dad was in the Department of Energy, so he would have some expertise in that area that the CIA could draw upon."

"I think both you and Willy are way off base."

"It was Willy's idea in the first place, and I thought he was out of it too, until I saw the computer material. Dad and Mom have been lying to us, Doug. Dad's not out looking for a job. He's doing something, and we don't know what it is. What's the explanation?"

"I don't have an explanation. Why don't you just go and ask Dad?"

"How can I ask him without admitting I've been spying on him?"

"Maybe he'll recruit you for the CIA, too."

Kara stepped back, annoyed. "You think it's all a

big joke, don't you? Well, I thought so too before this."

"I think I have work to do. So would you please leave?"

She looked at the steno pad on his lap. "What's that for?"

"English. I'm writing a diary."

"What are you going to say in it?"

"Good night, Kara!"

She opened the door and huffed. "Well, good night, John-boy."

18

Cindy Ballentine was in her room trying to discover the base angles of an isoceles triangle, trying to decide exactly what use she was going to make of the knowledge five, ten years into the future. There were so many things you did because you had to, and now all of the sudden she wanted to know why.

Her mother was on the phone. Her father was in the living room watching television. She supposed she could rush down and demand of her father whether it mattered if the angle of A was forty-five degrees or thirty-eight. "It matters because you're told that it matters," he would bark at her.

Obviously that would be the wrong way to go at it. Maybe she should just go down the stairs and ask sweetly if he could help her with her geometry. That would get him. Then she would say with all innocence, "But if a wise, understanding man such as you doesn't know how to find the angles, why should I even attempt to learn this?"

No. Then he would know he had been set up. She was already in enough trouble. It would have been easier if her parents could have decided if she was guilty of something or not, so they would know how to punish her and for what. But it was just such a set of crazy circumstances that they didn't know where to pin the blame. Should they punish her because she was alive?

"Cindy." The sound of her mother's voice coming like a guardian angel from beyond her door startled her.

"Yes, Mom?"

"May I come in?"

Cindy bent over her work. "Sure."

Mrs. Ballentine turned the knob and opened the door to the room that had been done over just last fall in yellow and white. She approached her daughter at the desk and peered over her shoulder. "What are you doing?"

"Geometry."

"Ugh! I hated geometry," she said with intense remembrance.

Cindy was surprised by her mother's honesty. "I hate it, too. Why do I have to take it?"

Her mother shrugged. "Because they say you have to take it."

Cindy let the nonsense of that sink in.

"That was Miss Pritcher on the phone."

Just what she needed. More trouble. "Oh?"

"She was quite upset. We had a long talk about your attitude."

Cindy groaned inwardly. Only adults used terms like "your attitude."

"I told her you were very upset about the accident, and she agreed with me that your behavior was quite out of the ordinary. For you. But she felt that, because the incident had taken place in front of the entire pom squad, you would have to be suspended for a month. I said that sounded fair. How does it strike you?"

Cindy's mind was churning, but she kept silent.

"Cindy?"

"Miss Pritcher—Miss Bitcher," she spat out.

"Cindy!"

"Oh, Mother, you don't understand anything."

"I understand that you don't call your teachers bitches."

"Everyone calls her Miss Bitcher."

"She's only trying to do what's best for you."

"Mother, can you really believe that?"

"Then tell me what I should believe."

Cindy shook her head. "I can't. You don't understand how life works."

"I think I remember some of it." The tone was a little frosty.

Cindy faced her mother squarely. "All right, then. Do you remember my most unhappy day? That's not counting the day Michelle got killed, of course."

Her mother thought back on it. There had been so many days of drama in her daughter's life that she couldn't pick out the worst one.

"It was the day I didn't get picked for junior varsity cheerleading."

"But then you got picked for pom squad."

"I said you wouldn't understand."

"Well, explain it to me."

"Why do you think some people get picked for cheerleading and some don't?"

"Because some cheer better?"

"No. That's not the way it works, Mom. There's the coach and the co-captains of senior varsity cheerleading. They decide. It doesn't matter how well you cheer, unless you're a real clutz. It matters how popular you are, what kind of rep you have. You could have an Olympic medal in cheerleading, if they gave one out, and still not be picked for the squad if you hadn't gone to the right parties or been seen with the right boys."

When her mother didn't say anything, she went on. "Everyone knows that's the way the system operates. When I didn't make j-v cheerleading, they were telling me I wasn't popular enough to make it. That I had to shape up my act. So I started seeing Charlie Sims because he had a big rep, which meant maybe I could make the cheerleading squad next year. They like cheerleaders who go with football players."

"But I thought you liked Charlie."

"He's okay."

"Oh, Cindy, to go out with someone just to make the cheerleading squad. Is it so important?"

"I used to think so."

"But the pom squad—"

"The pom squad is for second-raters. They're telling you you're popular but not that hot."

"I can't believe this."

"Well, believe it, Mother, because that's the way life is at Oakdale."

"But you went out with Doug Valvano. He's not on the football squad, certainly."

"Yeah. Everyone thinks he's a real drip. Everyone who matters."

"I thought he was rather nice."

"I thought he was nice, too," Cindy agreed with a sigh.

Her mother smiled uncertainly. "So what are you telling me?"

"I'm telling you, Mother, that I've spent enough of my life trying to be popular. It's not worth the effort. There are other things in life I want to try before I end up like Michelle."

"And what does all this have to do with Miss Pritcher?"

"Miss Pritcher thinks she can terrorize us by

threatening not to put us on the pom squad next year. Most of the girls feel that once they're off the pom squad, they're nothing. I no longer feel that way. I'm no longer willing to play Miss Pritcher's silly game."

Mrs. Ballentine smiled at her daughter. "You know, I think you're beginning to grow up. I also think, my dear, that there is a price you're going to have to pay for your decision. You might find some of your friends now turning their backs on you."

"There are other people in Oakdale besides my friends."

"Like Doug Valvano?"

"He's one of them," Cindy conceded.

Her mother stood up. "Well, you'll always be popular with me, Cindy," she assured her daughter.

Fine, Cindy thought, but it didn't help with her geometry.

19

Her mother's prediction of friends turning their backs on her proved only too prophetic when Cindy's newfound resolve not to go with the flow of her old crowd was tested. Nine days after the accident, the news filtered through Oakdale like flour through a sieve: Red Bucknell, who had awakened from his coma a few days earlier, was lying in bed sucking on chipped ice with his mother sitting beside him when in walked two state policemen. Then and there, Red Bucknell was charged with three counts of homicide with vehicle.

Homicide.

He willfully and recklessly had taken three lives.

Cindy watched as all of a sudden the Oakdale students turned into television lawyers. Homicide? Sure, but he could plea bargain it down to manslaughter. Homicide? But where was the weapon? Is a car a weapon? Certainly not like a gun, a knife, a stick even. And Red hadn't meant to kill anyone.

Kevin Dowling, senior class president, began circulating a petition protesting the decision to charge

Red with so serious a crime. Some of the students signed it automatically. Cindy had to give it more thought. She remembered how she had felt when she found out that Michelle was dead and Red was alive. Her anger had ignited within her. Now it was a quieter fire, but it burned still. It burned for Michelle. Cindy would not sign Kevin's petition.

"You've got to," Kevin urged. "After all, you were in the car. If you sign it, the police will really have second thoughts."

"That's another reason not to sign it," Cindy informed him. "How do I know I won't be called as a witness? I don't want to do anything prejudicial to the case."

"The case against Red?"

"There is a case against Red, Kevin. If Red hadn't been drinking, Michelle, Bob, and Ellen would still be alive."

Kevin took a step backward. "What's happened to you, Cindy?"

"I can't come up with automatic answers any more. I have to think things through. And what I think is that Red was wrong."

Even as she turned away from him, she could feel Kevin mouthing words against her. It made her weak in the knees and sick to her stomach. She knew that only weeks ago she would have given in to Kevin, just to keep in everyone's good graces. Now there was a new Cindy, more fragile, but perhaps stronger for it.

When Cindy considered it, she wished that Mr. Heald had banned the petition from the school. It was only being divisive. But the principal and the other administrators always took care never to violate even a suspected civil right. After all, living so near Washington, there were always too many lawyers who doubled as parents, too many lawyers looking for a cause célèbre.

Maybe she should speak to Mr. Heald. No. He never listened. He just mouthed platitudes. Like most adults. So the petition wars would go on.

The girls' swim team refused to sign Kevin's petition. Ellen was the best they had, but now, because of Red, she would always be remembered as that girl who died drunk.

The football team signed the petition. Red was one of them. Bob would have wanted them to stick together. Maybe there was no shame in a boy's dying drunk. Maybe that was the macho thing to do.

Cindy had a chance to assess their attitude when Charlie Sims confronted her about not signing the petition. He even threatened to drag her by the twisted arm over to the petition desk. He was smiling when he said it.

She shook her head in disbelief. "Charlie, you were the one who spoke to me so movingly about Bob only a few days ago, how he played the violin and everything. How can you just let his death go unpunished? If the driver were a stranger, would you let him go free? No, you guys would be over at that stranger's house with baseball bats."

"But he's not a stranger, Cindy," Charlie argued. "He's Red. And nothing's going to bring Bob back."

"So just forget about him?"

"I'm not forgetting about him."

"Oh, is that why you're supporting a petition to release his killer from criminal responsibility?"

"Don't confuse me with terms like 'criminal responsibility.' You stick with your friends. That's all I know."

"Whoever's left of them," she flung at him.

"Cindy, what's happened to you? Why are you being so argumentative all of the sudden?"

"Just because I say what I think for a change, that's being argumentative?"

"I understand. You're upset because you got kicked off the pom squad."

"Suspended."

"Sassing Miss Bitcher. Oh, oh, oh! Bad girl."

She smiled.

"That's more like it."

"Look, Charlie, you have your way of looking at things, I have mine. Let's just leave it at that with this petition."

"Okay, Cindy, but you're making a lot of enemies."

Later that same day she found that Charlie wasn't the only one worried about her popularity. She saw Doug just before lunch period was over. He was standing with a group of his friends, but she could tell he wasn't taking part in the conversation. He was not reacting to anything they were saying. When he saw her and she smiled, he detached himself from his friends and came to her.

"Have you met with the petition yet?" he asked, as if the petition were a demon locomotive bearing down on them.

She nodded. "I refused to sign, of course."

"Cindy!" he scolded.

"What?"

"Everybody's signing it."

"Did you?"

"Not on your life."

"A strange choice of words. Anyway, I told Kevin Dowling that I might have to testify in court so I couldn't sign."

"Something else to look forward to," Doug said.

"How's everything?" There was real concern in her voice.

"Do I look so down? I don't know." He shook his head. "I keep replaying the accident in my mind."

"Sounds familiar."

"It's like a nightmare I can't shake. I just see everything so vividly. And it comes no matter where I am, in class, walking home, doing homework."

"Comes unbidden."

"What?"

"Oh, English class. We're studying British poetry. 'Comes unbidden' seems to have been a phrase all could agree upon."

"English." He sighed. "I wish I had your teacher. I have to write that diary."

She smiled. "I'd love to read it."

"No one's ever going to read it," he promised, almost threatened.

"Not even your English teacher?"

"Not if I can help it. I've been too honest. I've got to write up a fake one to turn in."

"The day was bright, the sky was mellow."

"Yeah. May I borrow that? Hey, I know I'm being a real self-centered pain. How are things with you?"

She shrugged. "Okay."

"Okay? I heard you got kicked off the pom squad." He seemed taken aback when Cindy reacted angrily.

"Well, let me correct you on that," she said. "I was suspended. But I'm not planning to go back when my suspension is lifted. There are more important things in life than the pom squad."

"Like what?"

"Honestly, Doug, is that all you wanted to do, date a pom squad member?"

"Oh, Cindy, don't be silly. Anyone would want to date you."

She smiled, softened. "Do you think you can help me with geometry?"

"I haven't done any work since the accident," he confessed.

"What?"

"I'm failing everything."

"You're failing? But everyone calls you a grind."

"I thought I was a wimp."

"Well, okay, wimpy-grind." She smiled, teasing. But then she saw it was no laughing matter to Doug. "What are you going to do?"

He had no answer.

"You'd better start working."

But he didn't. Or at least Cindy assumed he hadn't because, a few weeks after her talk with him, she heard he was called down to the guidance office to discuss his failing grades.

20

Kara sat at the kitchen table listening to her parents berate her brother. "If you were having trouble with your studies, you should have come to us," Mrs. Valvano said.

Her mother had been devastated when the guidance counsellor called to say that Doug was getting D's and E's in everything except band and gym.

"You've always been a straight-A student," Mr. Valvano said with real anguish.

"What it is?" Mrs. Valvano demanded. "What's happened to you?"

Kara could have told them. She knew Doug hadn't been the same since the accident. Like the other day. She and Willy had been running, just an easy jog— conditioning, Willy called it—getting ready for the first track and field meet of the spring season, when Doug had come along. Well, they had come along him and passed him and circled back again. He had stared at them while they kept pace with his slow, methodical walking. Then he had asked, "What is the point of running?" Now if that wasn't the sign of a sick mind, what was?

But parents were slow in making this sort of connection. Like her father. All the time the evidence was piling up against him. She and Willy had gone down into the basement again when neither of her parents was at home. They had found the remnants of a short wave radio and an old headset.

"Look at how professionally this is done," Willy had said, as he picked up the headset with his pencil. "Your father must use it and then respray it with dust so it looks unused."

"I bet the radio doesn't even work," Kara challenged him.

Willy took up the glove. He fitted several of the loose tubes back into the chassis, plugged it in, and she heard the whining noise so familiar to those who watched old World War II movies on television. "Desperate times make desperate men," Willy had commented.

When she told Doug about it, he had just shrugged. He didn't even want to see the radio. Her brother, whom she should have been able to rely on, was being annoyingly no help at all.

After the discovery of the radio, she had stared at her father across the dining-room table, hoping she could make him feel guilty enough to confess. His response: "Jan, you'd better take Kara to the eye doctor. I think she's getting cross-eyed. She always seems to be looking at me."

Hopeless. Parents were absolutely hopeless when it came to the subtleties of life. Like making the connection between Doug's grades and the accident. Or maybe they did make the connection and just didn't want to speak about it. It was hard to tell, except the accident was definitely not a favorite topic of conversation around their home. She supposed discussing Doug's grades was a safe outlet.

Doug didn't defend himself. Well, how could he really? It's hard to defend D's and E's. He murmured an occasional response but he said nothing meaningful.

Of course they put restrictions on him. They grounded him. Which was sort of silly, as he hadn't gone out since the night of the accident, anyway. They told him he couldn't watch television except on the weekends. Not too bad, as they only let them watch one hour a day at most. Then they threatened to take away his radio if his marks didn't improve immediately. Now they were getting serious. Doug and his radio were inseparable.

Doug got up from the table and left the room, duly chastized. Or at least acting sensibly as if he were duly chastized. Her mother began to clean away the dishes, the worry lines in her face accentuated. She even seemed to be talking to herself; her lips moved and she shook her head occasionally.

Finally Mrs. Valvano noticed her daughter still sitting there. "Kara, do you know what's wrong with Doug?"

Kara shrugged. Despite the fact that he hadn't been much help to her lately, she didn't want to rat on her brother. After all, he had a mouth. If he had wanted to tell them what was wrong, he could have. Still and all, she didn't like to see her mother distressed. "You might check his diary," Kara suggested tentatively.

Her mother dropped the silverware back on the table. "Doug's keeping a diary?"

"Of course," Kara said, as if it were the most natural thing in the world for a fifteen-year-old boy to do. "It's an assignment from his English teacher. Doug must be taking it very seriously. He hides the diary in the second stack of his *Sports Illustrated*."

Mrs. Valvano stared at Kara in amazement. "How do you know all this?"

"Simple observation, my dear Watson."

"Have you read the diary?"

Kara was offended. "Do you think I'm a snoop or something?"

"You would make an excellent spy, Kara." Her mother gave her a knowing smile.

Kara said nothing. One spy in the family was certainly enough.

21

Doug had his radio on so loudly that, when his mother knocked on his door the first time, he didn't hear her. He had come right home from school intending to do some homework—mostly study for his biology test, so he wouldn't fail another one and have his parents even more upset at him. But his mind kept drifting until there'd been nothing for it but to take out the newest science fiction paperback and read himself into another world.

When his mother knocked a second time and called his name, he guiltily shoved the paperback into the top drawer of his desk, said, "Just a minute," and rose to open the door.

"Hi, Doug, how are you?"

"Hi, Mom. Had a good day?"

"May I come in for a moment?"

"Sure."

His mother sat on his desk chair while he perched on the edge of his bed. They looked at each other, waiting for the tension to disappear miraculously. But it didn't. "I don't really feel like making small talk, Doug," his mother finally said.

"Uh—did you want to discuss my grades again?"

"As I remember last night, it wasn't really a discussion. I was talking; your father was talking; you were saying nothing."

"I promised to try to do better," Doug reminded her.

"But you didn't tell us why you had let everything slip so."

"Well—I don't know."

"Maybe you do but you can't say it."

"I don't understand."

"Sometimes it's hard to find words for our deepest pain."

"Mom."

"All right. I'm not going to give you a lecture, or embarrass you by asking questions neither of us may want answered. But maybe there's another way for us to understand each other."

Doug didn't have the vaguest idea of what his mother was talking about.

"Kara says you keep a diary."

"The snoop!"

"No, Doug. She says she knows it's an English project you have. Is the diary the answer for us? Are there things in the diary that you feel you can't tell us? If we read them, would we understand what is happening to you a little bit better, especially since you seem unable or unwilling to tell us out loud?

"Your father and I want to help you," she went on

when he didn't answer. "We have been through a slightly similar experience. Maybe we can work it out together. If not, at least let us be more aware of what is happening to you."

"Are you demanding to see my diary?"

"No. Whether you give us the diary or not is a choice you'll have to make. I just thought you might not like to be so all alone any more."

His mother left the room and closed the door on him. Doug was upset. If she knew about the diary, she should have demanded to see it. She should have ordered him to turn it over. It wasn't fair that he had to be the one to make the decision. The diary was like a bleeding gut—his. Would a doctor wait for permission to offer emergency medical care?

He took the steno pad out of his stack of *Sports Illustrated*'s and flipped through it. How could he let anyone see how terrible his mind had become? But then a frightening thought occurred to him: What if he never got better? Could he go on this way for much longer?

It was not until the next morning, after another sleepless, restless night, that he made his decision. He left the diary between the pillows of his parents' bed after he was sure they had both left the house. That way, if he changed his mind during school hours, he could retrieve the diary as soon as he came home and no one would be the wiser.

Except he had detention for not having his homework for the fifth time in a row in history. And when he got home, Kara met him at the door with the news that she and Mom were going out for a night on the town, first Roy Rogers, then the record shop where Mom promised to buy her one album of her choice, as long as it wasn't a double album. Wasn't that a great surprise? Which all too shortly left Doug stranded with his father and the diary.

They were in the living room together. The house was as still as a grave while Mr. Valvano read Doug's words and Doug sat like a headstone across from him.

January 28. The last of the funerals was held, this one for Ellen. It's funny. Being so close to sharing such an intimate experience as death with these three people, here I didn't really know any of them well enough to go to their funerals.

Ellen's mother is quoted in the papers as saying this was "the Lord's will." Is she serious! If I were the Lord, I would be enraged to be accused of such stupidity. Do people really think that God goes around making other people drunk so that he can take a select few out of this world? I don't know the answers to any of the questions I am asking, but even I would not come up with such a preposterous interpretation of Ellen's untimely death.

January 30. Tom called this morning to let me know that Red had come completely around. He's no longer fading in and out of consciousness. The doctor thinks the only thing wrong with him now is his two broken legs.

Tom heard from his mother who heard from another mother who heard from Red's father that all the Bucknells were bemoaning Red's accident, as it set him back, maybe permanently, in his search for an athletic scholarship.

How is Red feeling? Is he feeling like I'm feeling? Does he wonder why he alone survived the crash? Is he happy about it? Or does he feel guilty? Does he say to himself, if only?

"If only" has become my favorite phrase. If only I hadn't gone out on that date. If only I had called Dad from Barbara's house. If only I had stood in front of the car and refused to let Red drive. If only I had been in the car, I would be dead now and I wouldn't be having these problems.

Cindy has the same sort of feelings. She told me. Only her nightmare isn't on that back road, it's at Barbara's house. She wishes now she had let me call Dad from there. We're both crazy.

Cindy cries a lot, she says, but she's glad she's alive. She went to Michelle's funeral and that helped. It helped her to distinguish between life and death and which she preferred.

Perhaps if I had gone to a funeral. Mom asked me if I wanted to go, but I was afraid. They would have accused me. I would have stood guilty of not saving their son, their daughter.

February 1. Red Bucknell has been charged with three counts of vehicular homicide. They say the police marched into his hospital room in Baltimore and, in front of his mother, charged him with murder.

The school is in an uproar. Kevin Dowling is passing around a petition protesting the charges. Funny thing for a student president to do. What about Michelle, Bob, and Ellen? Who's passing around a petition protesting their deaths?

All Red's friends are harassing everyone who will not sign the petition. I did not sign it. Well, it doesn't matter about me. They already think I'm a wimp and a chicken. Sam and my other friends didn't sign it either. They agree with the police. Red was culpable. Fatally negligent, I would call it.

Cindy didn't sign it. I think she is ruining all her chances of being voted most popular sophomore girl. But she doesn't seem to care. That's not like her.

I suppose all this comes down to the question of what is murder. Some say that Red driving a car drunk is the same thing as Red pointing a loaded gun at someone. A drunk driver makes a car a lethal weapon. But Red's friends claim it was an accident that could have happened to anyone. And in this case they might be right. First of all, when I refer to that night, don't I refer to it as "the accident"? Second, don't all teenagers drink? I mean, that's the game to be played. To see how far underaged you can be and still get your hands on some liquor. So what happened to Red could have happened to anyone. Therefore aren't we all guilty? So why should Red be singled out? Just because he had the misfortune to kill three people who were riding in the car with him?

The answer to this question is "I don't know." I don't know how many drinks it takes to impair judgment. When I drive, if after this I ever decide I should drive, I will not drink. I have determined that. It is not worth the risk.

I know what this makes me. More wimpy. I can accept myself as a wimp. I cannot accept myself as a killer.

February 3. Sam told a joke today. I started to smile, but then I remembered there were three who were not smiling because of what I did or did not do. I have not decided whether I am fit to join the land of the living yet. When I figure out why I survived, maybe I will.

February 5. Jon came up to me today and of-

fered me some reds, a trial sample. Even as I shook him off, I wondered. Jon joined the space academy in seventh grade. Before that he was on my soccer team. He was a pretty good forward. Aggressive. After he started taking those pills, he didn't see the point of kicking the soccer ball into the net for a goal. I wonder if he's happy as a space cadet? I think not. "Life's a bummer," was the quote put under his ninth-grade picture in the yearbook. Did he know before any of us what I'm finding out now?

February 7. Mr. Valdez made fun of me in class today for not getting my work done. I wanted to tell him I didn't see the point of studying. I don't really care about whether we should return to the gold standard or not. I don't really care about anything.

I feel as if I've been asleep since January 23. As if I've been buried? There seems no point in going through the motions of everyday life when some cataclysmic event can just wipe you off the face of the earth in one eternal second.

February 12. I come home from school. I go up to my room and think. I hear Mom and Dad and Kara in the house living an ordinary life. How can they go on as if nothing had happened.

I am alone in my room and afraid to sleep. I am afraid of my dreams. My nightmares. I want

135

someone to come in and comfort me in the dark, but I am too old to ask.

February 14. Last night I made a Valentine card for Cindy out of construction paper and pictures from magazines. Today I got to school early before her bus arrived. I slipped the card through one of the ventilation slots in her locker. I stood in the hallway and watched. She opened her locker and the card fell out. She and her friends squealed. They picked it up and read it. Then they giggled. It said, "I love you. Guess who?" She'll never know who sent it. Even though she speaks to me, I am so far away from everyone now.

February 20. Red's home from the hospital. The football squad went over to see him. He was lying in bed with casts on both legs. But he was in good spirits.

His parents have hired a lawyer for him. The lawyer is trying to speed up Red's trial, so no blemish hangs over "this fine young man." He wants Red to be rolled into court in a wheelchair with his legs straight forward in casts. That way the judge will think twice before he sentences him to anything more than probation. The lawyer says until after the trial Red shouldn't even be in the same room where liquor is served. This seems rather stupid to me. The liquor has already done its damage. And at least he can't drive with his legs in casts.

I hear Bob's mother and father are making a big stink about their son's death. They want the prosecution to throw the book at Red, lock him up forever. Bob was their only son. It's funny because I don't think if Bob were here that he would want all this stink made. He and Red were friends, after all. Still, maybe I am wrong. Maybe he wants to be alive. Maybe in death he is angry and avenging. He was a good guy. Quiet. He did not walk with the usual football swagger. They say his family is Shinto. I must read about that.

I am wondering about becoming religious. But I can't believe. It is too simple.

February 24. I am getting worried. The grades are starting to roll in, and I haven't gotten anything above a D. What are Mom and Dad going to say to me? They want me to go to college even though they don't have the money to put me through.

Coach "Clean Living" Rucker came up to me in gym today. He told me how he and Red's father grew up together. He told me what a great boy Red was, a credit to his teammates, a giant of the future, an all 'round good kid. Then he asked if I was going to testify against Red at the trial. I told him no one had spoken to me about the trial and, if I testify, it wouldn't be against anyone. I would just be telling the truth. I think I was stuttering. He knew I was scared. He pushed his nose right up against me like you see the coaches do on TV and he said, "The truth isn't always what you think it is. Red needs all the help he can get."

It got me angry. Really angry. I was boiling inside. I wanted to punch him. It felt so good to want to do something after so long of wanting to do nothing that I laughed right in his face. He looked startled and he backed off.

March 3. I am alone all the time now. I have fallen away from everyone. I don't want to belong any more.

March 9. What am I going to do about my grades! I don't think my parents are going to understand this. Even if I put it to them philosophically.

March 11. Help! Someone! All I want is for this to STOP!!!

22

Mr. Valvano finished reading the diary. He held the steno pad on his knee as if it were an open wound that was bleeding all over him. "This is sick, Doug," he finally pronounced.

"May I have it back now, please?" Doug asked very calmly.

"Not yet."

"It's mine."

"Yes. I know it's yours. Doug?" His father sat silently for a minute with his son's name hanging between them. "Why didn't you come to us? Why didn't you talk to us about your feelings?"

"I came to you and you said everything was going to be okay. Well, it never got to be okay."

"You've let yourself become obsessed with this."

"Wouldn't you be obsessed if you thought you could have saved three people and you didn't?"

"Look! You did all you could. You did all that was humanly possible for a fifteen-year-old boy. And we are very proud of you. You knew right from wrong and you chose right for yourself. And the girl you were responsible for. You're not God, Doug. You can't control other lives."

"You would have saved them all."

"I don't know what I would have done."

Be perfect, Doug silently begged his father.

"No one knows what he would do in a situation like this until it actually happens. You had your wits about you. Frankly, that's more than most people would have had." His father was frowning. What isometrics. "Look, Doug, I know this is a cliché, but time heals all."

"Time? What's the good of time?" Doug exploded. "Time isn't endless. Somewhere it runs out and then we die. So what's the point of going on, especially in such pain?"

His father actually laughed at this. "That's the sort of question you ask at forty, not at fifteen. You have your whole life to look forward to."

Doug shrugged.

"Interpret the shrug, please," his father said.

"I don't know what sort of life I have to look forward to."

"A good life."

"Oh, sure. Like you?"

"What's that supposed to mean?"

"Oh, Dad, come on. Do you think Kara and I haven't seen you and Mom struggling over the past year? Here you are, you're forty-two. You worked at a job for so many years, then one day you're out with not even a thank you because you're just a bureaucrat, a moving target. You've got a house to pay for and us to feed, clothes to buy, and no money coming in. You get up in the morning, get dressed in a business suit, you're out day after day looking for work, but no one will hire you. At forty-two you're on the waste heap of our society. And after this past year, you're sitting here telling me life is worth living?" Doug, who had just let his words fly across the room, was now horrified to meet his father's eyes and find hurt in them.

"Oh, Doug, what an indictment."

"I didn't mean—"

"I know. You didn't mean to hurt me. You're probably surprised that adults can be hurt, your parents especially, since they've been taking crap from you and your sister ever since you were born. I'm sorry that you think my life adds up to a big fat zero."

"I didn't say that," Doug protested vehemently.

"Let me tell you something about life, Doug, that you'd better learn right now. It isn't easy. It's like those horror movies you're always watching. When you least expect it, something explodes from the darkness to kick your guts out. And, if we're going to have an adult conversation, I'm willing to confess that when I lost my job, I thought the world had come to an end. I saw myself as an absolute failure. All of a sudden, *whamo,* there was nothing left of me."

141

After a moment he went on. "It takes a while to get over something like that, to realize you are more than your job—a job—any job. It takes time. The very thing you mock. Now when I look back on losing my job, I think sometimes in my most optimistic moments that it might have been the best thing that ever happened to me. You see, Doug, man is a creative animal. He learns from crises, from obstacles strewn in his path. He circles them, he surmounts them, he overcomes.

"Since I've lost my job, I've gone off in an entirely new direction, one that I am enjoying tremendously."

Doug smiled. "What is it you're doing, Dad?" he asked, curious for Kara's sake.

"I'd rather not say until everything is settled. I don't want to brag about what hasn't happened yet. Time hasn't healed me that completely. Like touching a hot stove, I remember the hurt. You, also, my son, will be able to go on living, whether you believe me now or not. But you also will remember the hurt. That is the price we pay for being human, for having the capacity to learn from our mistakes, from our own and the tragedies of others.

"There is no life without pain, Doug. Growing up, being grown-up, both have their terrible moments. But we get through them. And there are good times, aren't there?"

"Not lately."

His father smiled. "But will you hold on long enough to reach some happier plateau? Can you?"

Doug stared down at his hands and made no reply. His father rose and came over to sit next to him on the couch. Slowly, his father put his arms around Doug and hugged him tight.

Doug cried. He cried freely and for a long time. But he thought it was okay to cry because his father was crying with him.

23

The next morning Doug awoke feeling somehow renewed. Life looked different to him. He no longer felt
that he alone bore the enormous weight of the world.
His father also carried a burden. And others. Each, he
realized, struggled with his own pain. And always so
silently. He had been selfish not to see that before. He
had thought of the accident only in terms of how it
affected him, not how it affected the others—parents,
friends, Cindy.

His bus reached school before hers did. He waited
outside as the March winds whipped rain clouds
across the heavens. It was cold. He wore neither hat
nor gloves. By the time her bus arrived, he could feel
his nose dripping. He must have looked great, but she
smiled when she saw him.

"I wanted to tell you," he said, as she bundled
quickly into the building so the wind could not flip her
hair too fiercely out of place, "I know you probably no
longer care, but I think I'm going to get over this."
Doug could see that Cindy was puzzled by this statement and its implications.

"Of course I care," she said, looking a little hurt.

"Well, I know I've been a—a—"

"Wimp."

"Lately," he added agreeably.

They both laughed. Comfortable with each other, they walked down the hallway.

"So why this change?" she asked.

"I talked to my father last night. I hadn't before. I mean really talked."

She nodded. Was she remembering his father in the car that night?

"It wasn't what he said so much as how he said it. You see, he said something real to me. Not what parents usually says. He didn't hit me with what ought to be; he talked about what really is."

Cindy listened, nodding.

"Now I'm sort of looking at the situation differently. It's like I've fallen to the bottom of a well, come face to face with my monsters, and am climbing back up."

"I'm glad."

"Of course, I might fall down again," Doug admitted.

"No."

"The first person I thought about when I was zapped by this miraculous revelation that I might survive was you. I've left you stranded."

She laughed at that. "I've left you swamped."

"What do you mean?" he asked.

"I heard about your being called down to the guidance office."

"Oh, that." He groaned.

They were almost at her locker now. When Doug
looked up, he saw Charlie Sims waiting for her. He
was suddenly unaccountably jealous. "Is that part of
your recovery program?" he asked without thinking.

She smiled michievously. "There's no law saying
Charlie can't stand by my locker."

"There ought to be. Are you going out with him?"

"I can't go out with him. I'm still grounded."

"Well, at least your father has that much sense."

She giggled. He remembered why he had asked her
to the Snow Ball.

"Listen, don't be surprised if I call you in a few
days," she said, her back turned on Charlie.

He frowned. She swiveled away from him and
greeted Charlie effusively. Call him in a few days?
What was she planning? He wondered, he worried, he
fretted. He cherished the suspense.

"What was that all about?" Charlie asked Cindy,
after Doug was out of sight.

"Nothing."

"Nothing?"

"We just talked."

"About what?" Charlie demanded.

"About things."

He gave up. "How's everything with your parents?"

She was puzzled. "Fine. Why do you ask?"

"Are you still grounded?"

"Yes. Well—" Cindy chided herself for letting the truth seep into her answer. But Charlie would have to know anyway.

"Well, what?"

"They might end it in a few days."

"That's great! Are they going to end it in time for the Sadie Hawkins' dance?"

She looked down at her toes. "Probably."

"Well?"

She swore silently at him. Charlie was being really obtuse. "Haven't you been seeing a lot of Lisa Nevins lately?"

"Yeah. She asked me to the dance."

Cindy breathed a sigh of relief. "That's great!" she exclaimed, truly happy.

"I told her I'd have to let her know. I felt sure your parents would have to relent sooner or later."

"Oh, Charlie, you should go with Lisa since she asked you."

"Hey, she was only filling in for you."

"I'm sure *she* didn't know that."

Charlie stepped closer. "Are you trying to tell me you don't want to ask me to the dance?"

Cindy knew the time for hemming and hawing had passed. "It's not that I don't want to ask you. It's just that there's someone I have to ask first." She felt an immediate blast of frigid air between them.

"Not Doug Valvano."

She made a thin line of her lips.

"Cindy, you can't be serious. What do you figure you owe the guy—another date because your first one turned out so rotten?"

She could have slapped him. "I'm asking Doug because I like him, because he's human, and has human emotions."

"And I don't?"

"You do, Charlie, but you never let anyone see them."

"You know, you've become weird. Really weird."

She sighed.

"If you ask Doug Valvano to the Sadie Hawkins' dance, don't ever expect to see me again."

"Okay."

"Just like that! We had some fun times together."

"Some of them were a lot of fun. Some of them were only so-so," she struck back at him.

He shook his head. "I can't talk to you any more, Cindy. You've changed."

Thank God, she murmured to herself.

"Well, I guess I'll go with Lisa Nevins."

"Have a good time, Charlie."

"Yeah. You, too, I guess."

He backed away from her. Then he turned and walked away.

24

Doug was home alone after school, examining the package he had received that day in the mail. It contained all sorts of seeds for the garden he planted each spring—radishes, cucumbers, peas, cabbages, okra, squash. The tomatoes he would buy as plants. It was easier than growing them from seed.

He hadn't ordered any flower seeds. If he had known he would become friends with Cindy Ballentine, he might have. It would have been nice to present her with a bouquet from his own garden. What had she meant: don't be surprised if she called? He smiled.

He heard a car pull into the driveway. It must be his mother with Willy and Kara, home from the first track meet of the season. He got up and opened the door for them. "First, eight-hundred meter!" Kara shouted proudly at him.

Doug grinned. "How did it go with you, Willy?" Willy looked glum. Doug guessed he had asked the wrong question.

Mrs. Valvano was walking toward the house. "Willy was the star of the relays. If it weren't for Willy, Kennedy wouldn't have racked up as many points as it did."

"Then why is he looking so down?" Doug asked.

"The fifteen-hundred meter didn't go as planned."

"I lost," Willy almost growled. "And to a kid younger and two inches shorter. The humiliation of it! Do you realize how I felt?"

"Only too well," Doug assured him. He remembered his days on the junior-high softball team, all his teammates waiting, praying for a hit. Then the umpire calling, "Strike three"; and he'd had to return to the bench where the coach and everyone sat, staring at him.

Willy, Kara, and Mrs. Valvano followed him into the kitchen where the seed packets were still spread on the table. "Are you sure you don't mind my staying for dinner, Mrs. Valvano?" Willy asked.

"Of course I'm sure. No reason why you should stay home alone and have leftover casserole when you can have leftover casserole here." She sorted quickly through the mail. "The bank statement," she groaned. "My very favorite."

Doug cleared off the table while Willy and Kara were noisily getting something to drink. He almost didn't hear his mother when she said, "That's funny."

"What's funny, Mom?"

"We have extra money in our checking account."

"That's good."

"That's not good, Doug. It doesn't belong to us."

150

"What doesn't belong to us, Mom?" Kara came over to ask.

"We have two deposits of over a thousand dollars each in this month's account. I certainly didn't make them." She checked her watch. "Too late to call the bank today. I'll have to do it tomorrow, and then it will take them weeks to straighten it out."

"Why call them? Maybe it's a gift from a secret admirer," Willy suggested.

She laughed. "If only I were that lucky. No, we'll have to give it back. Would you kids put the food in the oven and set the table? I'm going up to change."

"Too bad," Kara said, taking the casserole out of the refrigerator. "We could have used the money."

"You know, your mother is very uptight morally. It must be hard living with her sometimes."

"Yeah. It is," Kara agreed.

Willy was folding the napkins when he suddenly stopped. "Of course!" he exclaimed. "I told you they couldn't tell their wives."

"You think the money is my father's?" Doug asked. "Don't you?"

"Mom said it was a mistake," Kara reminded him.

" 'Cause your mother doesn't know. Just like I told you she wouldn't."

"You're full of it, Willy," Doug told him.

"You know, it seems to me that everyone in this family is afraid to face the truth. It's not as if it's a dishonorable thing to work for the CIA. I bet they have a great travel allowance."

"Dad never goes anyplace," Kara informed Willy.

"Yet." He looked at them. "Add it all up: The locked briefcase, the computer printout, the radio, the days he spends away from home supposedly looking for a job, the extra money in the checking account. *If* it's not the CIA, then what is it?"

"I don't know," Kara said, "but I'm going to find out."

Mr. Valvano walked in the door at five fifteen and found his family, plus Willy, waiting for him. He looked so happy to be home, Doug thought. How could he know they were actually a posse of vigilantes.

Dinner proceeded normally enough. Mr. and Mrs. Valvano, Kara, Willy, and Doug sat around a butcher block table, eating Eggplant Italia, Mr. Valvano's latest creation. "I'm sure this is healthy," Willy managed to say when he found out which vegetable he was dealing with.

Mr. Valvano politely asked about the track meet and listened with interest and some sympathy while Willy explained exactly how the shorter kid outran him.

Doug outlined his plans for this year's garden, and his mother was extremely pleased. "Do you know, I still have some jars of your tomatoes left from last year."

"Really?"

Kara harumphed, demanding some attention.

"Yes, Kara?" Mr. Valvano inquired, as he helped himself to some more of the casserole, though everyone else was just picking at it.

"Mom received an interesting piece of mail today, too."

Mr. Valvano turned to his wife. "The bank statement," she said. "I was going to show it to you after dinner. That computer! We have over two thousand dollars *extra* deposited in our account this month. I'm going to call them tomorrow—"

"I wouldn't do that, Jan."

Willy glanced significantly at Kara.

"Tony, we just can't keep the money."

"Oh, yes, we can."

Mrs. Valvano jumped up and got the bank statement. She waved it under her husband's nose. "You mean you know something about this?"

He moved his head back so he could see the figures. "Yes."

"You do?"

"Yes."

"What?"

"It's ours, Jan."

"What!" This time she screeched it. "What have you been up to?"

"We'll discuss it later."

"No!" Kara jumped up, nearly knocking her water glass to the floor. "Let's discuss it now!"

"Kara!" her mother exclaimed in amazement.

"Please," Kara added. Then, "Willy thinks you're a spy," she blurted.

"A what!" her mother and father said at the same time.

"Willy said—"

"I think I'll have another helping of that delicious Eggplant Italia, Mr. Valvano," Willy said quickly.

"What exactly did you say, Willy?" Mr. Valvano asked, as he plopped more food on Willy's plate.

"I thought you were with the CIA," Willy mumbled.

Mr. Valvano looked stunned. "How did Sherlock Holmes Nathan come to that conclusion?"

Willy was blushing. Doug decided to rescue him. "It was your locked briefcase more than anything, Dad," he explained. "And the fact that you left the house each day dressed up as if you had someplace to go."

"And the computer printout of the Russian gas fields in your briefcase," Kara put in.

"The Russian—my briefcase? So that's what you two were doing down there in the basement. And all the time I thought you and Willy were playing Spin the Bottle."

"Dad, please!" Kara joined Willy in turning red.

"What were you doing, Dad?" Doug asked.

"Well. Since this story looks as if it will have a happy ending, I guess there's no harm in telling you now. Is there, Jan?"

"It's your decision," she told him.

"For a time, after I lost my job, I was leaving the house, looking for another job. It was hopeless with so many people out of work and looking, too—hopeless and, frankly, humiliating. So your mother and I decided to take a gamble. It was obvious that I wasn't going to find another job as a middle level manager with the government or anyone else. Not at forty-two years of age. So we took some of our savings and used it to pay my tuition at the Compu-Education Center. For the past eight months I have been learning all about programing and systems analysis. That's where the computer printouts came from. I kept my briefcase locked because I didn't want anyone snooping around it. You have to remember that it's been twenty years since I attended school, and I really didn't know if I could cut it. But my instructors thought I was managing quite well. Three months ago they arranged an internship for me at Universal Communications in its satellite division. One month ago"—he turned to his wife—"Universal Communications changed my status from intern to salaried professional. Ergo, the two thousand in the checking account."

Mrs. Valvano clapped her hands with joy. "Why didn't you tell me?"

"What if they had changed it back to intern?"

"Oh, Tony, I am just so proud of you!"

"You know, Jan, I'm sort of happy with myself."

They smiled at each other, then rose together from the table. "You kids clean up," Mrs. Valvano sug-

155

gested. "Your father and I are going out for a hamburger. To celebrate."

Doug, Kara, and Willy sat in silence until they heard the car pull out of the driveway.

"I think, if we're very careful, we should be able to wrap the Eggplant Italia in old newspapers and dispose of it so Dad never has to know," Doug suggested.

"CIA!" Kara shot at Willy.

"I wasn't far off," Willy pointed out. "Universal Communications, satellite division? How do you know it doesn't have some CIA connections? The Pretender often works undercover like that. Why, I remember the time he was sent to Iran as a Bible salesman. Boy, that was a tough one. He had to leave in a hurry without his invoices."

"Willy, have you ever thought of returning to the state nature intended for you—illiteracy?"

"On the other hand, we could finish the Eggplant Italia and miss school tomorrow," Doug ventured. But his sister and Willy weren't listening to him. They had left the kitchen to resume their argument in the living room. The mess was left for him to clear away. But for once he didn't mind. His father had a job; his mother was happy; Cindy was going to call him. What more could a fellow ask? Except perhaps that his mother would now resume the cooking.

25

Cindy sat by the telephone and stared at it. Is this what boys went through, she wondered, every time they had to ask for a date?

Maybe Doug didn't want to go out with her. Then she would really be making a fool of herself. And there wouldn't be anyone else to ask. Certainly not Charlie. If Doug refused her, Charlie would see she wasn't at the dance and know what had happened. He would spread it around that even Doug Valvano wouldn't go out with Cindy Ballentine. Great.

But she thought Doug liked her. He gave every indication of liking her, if looks meant anything. They shared something together. Not just the accident. They could talk, communicate, understand each other. Doug was a friend.

So why was she afraid to call him? Because he would turn her down. She just knew he would.

Courage, she told herself. She picked up the phone and immediately proceeded to misdial. She pushed the button down before it could ring at the other end and shook her head. Fingers, work right, she ordered. She would dial again.

It rang three times. Was nobody home? "Hello?" It was a girl's voice. Doug's sister?

"Hello, may I speak to Doug, please?" Cindy asked.

"Hey, Doug," Cindy heard the girl call. "It's someone feminine." She still had a chance to hang up, but the phone stuck, as if glued to her ear.

"Hello?"

"Doug?"

"Yes."

"It's Cindy."

"Cindy, hi!"

"Well, I told you I'd call."

The silence hung between them, each expecting the other to go on. "What did you call about?" Doug finally managed to ask.

"Um, well, uh—"

"Geometry? I have my notes from last year. Weren't you in advanced math?"

"Not exactly. Yes, well I did call about geometry."

"Okay."

"Um—well—" This was silly. If she didn't watch it, she really would be discussing her problems with angles. That was the last thing she wanted to talk about. She had enough geometry in class. "Doug, I didn't call about math," she burst out.

"Oh?"

"I wanted to know—well—would you like to go to the Sadie Hawkins' dance with me?"

The phone went dead. Or at least he wasn't answering. Maybe they had been disconnected. There was silence. "Doug?"

"You want *me* to go to the Sadie Hawkins' dance with you?"

"Well, yes. That's why I asked. Oh, I suppose you're already going with Valerie Brown?"

He laughed. "Cindy, I'd love to go with you."

"You would!"

"I'm just humbled that anyone so wonderful as you would ask me."

She blushed and felt incredibly desirable. "Are you reading that out of a book?"

"No!"

"Well, I'm glad you agreed to go with me because I've already asked my father if he could drive us."

"Oh, oh."

She laughed. "He's looking forward to it."

"I bet."

"So we'll pick you up at eight, okay?"

"Okay. I'll see you in school before that."

"Right. 'Bye, Doug."

" 'Night, Cindy."

She put down the phone and breathed a sigh of relief. That wasn't as hard as she'd thought it was going to be. However, it wasn't that easy either. She was glad the Sadie Hawkins' dance only came once a year.

After putting the phone down, Doug just leaned against the kitchen wall and smiled.

"What was that all about?" Kara asked nosily.

"Cindy Ballentine just asked me to the Sadie Hawkins' dance," Doug bragged.

"You're kidding! You?"

He ignored her, little twerp that she was, and marched up the stairs. At the top, his mother called out from her room. He went to her.

"Who was that?" she asked.

"Cindy. I'm going to the Sadie Hawkins' dance with her."

Mrs. Valvano looked at her son, pleased and worried at the same time. "My, my," was all she said. There was an unspoken question in her eyes.

"Her father's driving," Doug said, as if he had read her mind.

"Now I feel a lot better about your date with Cindy," she replied with a smile.

Doug smiled back at her, but his thoughts were not so pleasant. It was easy for his mother to feel better about Mr. Ballentine's driving them. She had never met him. Doug had. And it was an experience he remembered all too well, one that he did not want to repeat.

26

Doug didn't go out of his way to let everyone at Oakdale know he was going to the Sadie Hawkins' dance with Cindy. He just told a few friends. They did the rest. It pleased him to be suddenly the object of envy. Though he heard that Charlie Sims had made a comment about Cindy's being really hard up. "The old green eyes of jealousy," as Sam put it.

However there was one drawback to this date with Cindy: the driver. He dreaded that meeting. How could he face her father; what would he say? He tried, "Hello, Mr. Ballentine, nice evening, isn't it?" He practiced the line over and over again, but it never came out smoothly. His voice had a certain squeak to it when he came to the "Mr. Ballentine." And besides, what if it rained? He could hardly say, "Hello, Mr. Ballentine, nice evening, isn't it?" if it were raining.

He called Cindy and tried to arrange it so that his father drove both ways, or at least one way. But Cindy said that was impossible, that her father insisted on driving her wherever she went now.

Saturday night rolled around and so did Cindy, at

about ten after eight. Doug had stood with his nose pressed against the windowpane, watching for her. She obviously wanted to be fashionably late to the dance.

Doug did not plan to wait for Cindy to get out and come to the door to fetch him. As soon as he saw the car pull to a stop he yelled a quick farewell to anyone within earshot and rushed out to greet his date. Cindy had the passenger door open. Doug slid in and managed not to close the door tightly enough. He had to reopen it and slam it.

"Evening, Mr. Ballentine. Nice evening, isn't it?"

"It's foggy out," Mr. Ballentine growled.

"But a pleasant mist. Good for the complexion," Doug returned hopefully.

Cindy crumpled in her seat with silent giggles.

"I mean, my mother always says—is always saying—that moisture in the air is good for the complexion. Not only good for our complexions, I should imagine, but think of the cosmic implications of the lack of moisture."

Doug, now feeling he had made a complete fool of himself, sat silently while Mr. Ballentine drove surely to the gym entrance of Oakdale High School. There Doug got out and held the door open for Cindy.

"Make sure you're out here by eleven o'clock," Mr. Ballentine warned them.

Together Doug and Cindy managed to slam the door shut the first time.

"Whew, did I blow that," Doug said, as Mr. Ballentine drove away.

"It could have been worse," Cindy cheered him. "At least you shut up after that stupid remark about the cosmic significance of moisture." She laughed and they went into the gym.

The Sadie Hawkins' dance was one of Oakdale High's famous theme dances. Last year the theme had been the Sixties and everyone had to come looking militantly spaced-out. This year the theme was country. Doug didn't own much country and western gear. But he wore a plaid flannel shirt and jeans held up with a thick leather belt. Around his neck he had tied a red bandanna that Kara used as a sweatband in the summer. He'd wanted to top his outfit off with a cowboy hat, but the only cowboy hat he owned was a straw one that his father had bought for him when he was eight.

Cindy was the stunner, Doug decided. She had on a plaid shirt, a jeans skirt, a fringed vest, and white cowboy boots with purple stars and flowers.

"Where did you get those boots?" he asked her as they waited in line to turn in their tickets and have their hands stamped.

"Baby-sitting money. They're terribly uncomfortable," she confided. "But everyone is wearing them."

Doug felt a twinge of sympathy for Cindy's being a girl and having to wear things just because they were fashionable. But then he thought, well, she had a choice. She could spend her time looking like Kara, changing between her jeans and her jogging suits. He was glad Cindy wasn't like Kara. Kara was pretty, but she still had a lot of growing up to do in the femininity department.

When they got out onto the dance floor, Doug saw that Cindy was right about the "gals" wearing cowboy boots, and, further, the "guys" were wearing them too. He tried to hide his white Nikes under the length of his jeans.

The loudspeakers were radiating "Stand By Your Man." Cindy pulled Doug closer and they began to dance. The rhythm of the song was all wrong for Doug's style of dancing, or lack of it. But Cindy didn't seem to mind.

"Hey!" she exclaimed suddenly, loud enough for him to hear over the music. "Thanks for the Valentine."

He blushed. "How did you know?"

"Oh, I could tell. Nobody else would have taken the time to handmake me one."

"Why? How many Valentines did you get?"

"Nine. And you?"

"None. Hey, wait. Kara gave me one."

"That's all right. Your favorite Valerie Brown got twenty."

"I didn't send her one."

"I thought you sort of went for Valerie."

"I did. But times change."

She smiled and sank closer to his heart.

At nine o'clock the whine of country music, which would have driven him out onto the streets if Cindy hadn't been in his arms, droned to a halt. A platform had been set up and on it sat a fiddler and a banjo player. Holding a tamborine was an old man in blue denims and red suspenders. "'Evening, ladies, 'evening gents," he called softly. "You buckaroos out there, grab your gals and form squares."

The whole gymnasium froze. Cindy whispered to Doug, "Patty said there would be entertainment, but she didn't say it would be us."

"I haven't square danced since seventh grade," Doug panicked.

"Come on, cowpokes. Corral them womenfolk and form them squares."

"We'll have to send him to Miss Baseheart for remedial English."

"My father's not coming till eleven."

"We'd better find a square, then."

They turned out to be couple Number Three, an innocuous position from which they managed to duck for the oyster and dive for the clam without butting heads with couple Number One. By accomplishing that feat, they were ready for the Texas Star.

Square dancing turned out to be so much fun that

they all forgot they should be hating it, that any kind of folk dancing was only for weird people. This caller wasn't anything like their former gym teacher, who had barked the steps out as if they were orders for NATO maneuvers. There was square dancing, then contra dancing. There were reels that they hadn't danced since fourth grade, and circle dances where the Old Geezers, as the group was called, tried to teach the young suburbanites how to clog. With all those cowboy boots, it made a great sound. The gym would probably never be the same again. By the time the band struck up "Good Night, Ladies," the Old Geezers had worn out their young charges.

Cindy looked up at the clock above the basketball hoop. "Five after. Daddy will be furious."

As they were making an effort to grab their coats, Suzie Evans called to them. "Hey, Cindy, you want to go out with us to Southies' Bar?"

Doug's heart froze.

"No, thanks," Cindy replied. "My father's waiting for us."

Doug studied Suzie and the group she was with. Were any of their names going to be in the paper tomorrow?

Cindy pulled him away and out to the circular drive where her father was waiting along with a few other parents.

"What's wrong with you, Cindy?" her father asked

out the car window. "You're walking funny."

Doug was upset that he hadn't noticed. "What's the matter?" he asked, and was surprised to see she looked embarrassed.

"This is the first time I've worn these cowboy boots. My toes are numb and I think my heels are bloody."

Doug laughed.

"It's all right for you. You had on sneakers." She poked him in the ribs. "But we had fun, didn't we?"

"You know, Cindy, I really did have fun."

He said it so positively that she sighed with happiness.

It was nice to have plain old fun again. It was nice to be normal.

27

Doug spent Sunday planning and plotting. There had to be a way for him to spend more time with Cindy. Away from parents driving. Away from other kids at school. Away from the pressure of bells ringing, signifying when they could talk, when they couldn't. Just alone together. By Monday morning he thought he had found it.

He waited for Cindy's bus to roll in. Perhaps it wasn't smart to be overanxious, but now that everyone knew Cindy wasn't grounded any more, there would be others waiting to ask her out.

She came off the bus and seemed startled to see him. She had on a Monday morning face, through with the weekend but not quite ready for school.

"Do you have a bike?" he asked her, forgetting even to say hello.

Nonplused, she answered, "I have a bike. I haven't ridden it since last summer. Why?"

"I thought maybe next Saturday you could bike over to my place. I have to work in my garden for a couple of hours, but then we could ride over to Northwood.

My sister's in a track meet there that afternoon."

Cindy walked past him, almost, into the school. He followed like a puppy. He was glad to see she wasn't limping from Saturday night's dance. They walked, one following the other, all the way to Cindy's locker. "Work in your garden?" she turned to ask.

"Sure. It's a lot of fun." He tried to sound convincing.

She made a face.

"Well, maybe you could just sit and watch," he compromised. "The track meet should be fun."

"Yes." She nodded. "Okay."

"You'll come?"

"Yes. Why not?"

Well, even if her enthusiasm wasn't overwhelming, it might grow as the weekend neared. At least, that was Doug's hope as he walked back down the hall.

He met Sam Rosen along their row of lockers just as the first bell rang. He let Sam in on the good news while he hurriedly fumbled with his lock.

"You have all the luck," Sam said admiringly.

"It's not luck, Sam, it's charm," Doug informed him.

He got his books and was set for first period, which was good because the halls were clearing rapidly. He was walking off with Sam toward homeroom when he noticed wheels and a red blur traveling down the main hallway toward the office. He stopped and stared open mouthed after the wheelchair.

"Yeah," Sam said. "He's back."

Red Bucknell, casts and all, had returned to Oakdale High.

Why? Doug asked himself as the week progressed. Why had Red returned, bringing with him the nightmare from which Doug had spent months trying to escape?

Trying to escape? He thought he had escaped, that it was all over. He thought after the talk with his father, after the dance with Cindy, after the coming of spring when everything is renewed, that his life too would become green again and rich. He had a chance for that. Until Red Bucknell came back to school.

Now he was stuck in winter. Stuck on the night of January 23.

Trapped. The corridors of Oakdale became a maze in which he tried to avoid the dreaded wheelchair. He didn't know what he would do if he had to come face to face with Red Bucknell. And he didn't want to find out.

By the time the weekend came, he had almost forgotten his date with Cindy and the pleasurable anticipation he had experienced early Monday morning, before he knew Red was back at school.

But Cindy had not forgotten. She asked what time

she should come. In a fog he told her about eleven.

Eleven on the dot Saturday morning, she pedaled up to his house and led her ten-speed around to the back where Doug was already working in the garden. He was wearing boots, and, as she wandered over to him, it was plain to see why. He was in the middle of a pile of rotting leaves, trying to clear the ground by shoveling them into a huge black plastic bag.

"You want me to help with that?" she asked.

Startled, he looked up as if he had not expected to see her.

"Do you want me to be here?" she wondered.

Slowly he left the garden. He came over to her and, without any greeting, said, "It's Red."

"I know." She understood. "When I first saw him it was like someone walking over my grave."

"Rolling over is more like it," Doug corrected her.

She smiled.

"Why did he have to come back! Just to haunt us?"

"The trial's set for June 28," she told him.

"I know."

"Then you should know why Red came back," she chided. "His lawyer wants him to graduate from high school and be accepted into college, any college, so that the judge would have less reason to send him to jail, so that the judge would think twice about ruining the life of this outstanding, this promising young man."

"Have you seen him?" Doug asked. "I mean, to talk to?"

"Yes. I said hello."

"And what did he say?"

"He said, 'Hi, Cindy, how's it going?' "

"Deep. Does he know you're going to testify against him?"

Cindy hesitated before answering.

"The prosecutor called my dad and said maybe I wouldn't be called because I had wanted to stay in the car with Red. They think that the defense will use the argument that if I wanted to stay in the car with Red driving, he couldn't have been that drunk."

"But they have his blood tests and everything."

"Yes," Cindy agreed. "He was well over the legal limit."

"I haven't seen him yet."

"I know. He knows, too. He knows you've been avoiding him."

"It's true," Doug admitted.

"Don't worry about it, Doug. Don't think about it so much."

"Aren't you thinking about it?"

"Less than before," she said carefully. "I'm angry at Red. I don't think you are. I think instead you're angry at yourself."

"Why should I be?"

172

"That's just the point, isn't it?" Her eyes held his.
"There's no reason for you to be angry at yourself."
He turned away and she reached to catch his arm.
"Let's have fun today," she almost ordered. "Like you
promised me on Monday."

He smiled. "Okay. I'll give it a try. We shall banish
Red from our presence. Let him haunt someone else.
At least for today."

28

It occurred to Doug after the first half hour of working alongside her that Cindy wasn't much of a gardener. He told her to hold up the plastic bag. But every time he got ready to shovel the compost in, she dropped the edges. They were making very little progress.

When he finally cleared enough of a strip to spade it and plant a row of peas, she didn't even want to cover the seeds with soil. "My nails," she explained.

"Haven't you ever had anything to do with gardening before?" he asked her.

"I played 'The Happy Farmer' on the piano. Isn't it time for the track meet?"

Doug checked the sun while she checked her watch. His parents had left with Kara to pick up Willy about half an hour ago, because Willy's mother was working and couldn't make it until later. The meet wouldn't start until two and his mother had left some sandwiches in the refrigerator for them. But it would be just as easy to stop off at McDonald's on the way to Northwood. He knew Cindy would like that better. She came into the house with him while he washed up. Then they mounted their bikes and started off.

By the time they reached Northwood's field, the center seats of the bleachers were all filled by parents and loyal friends. Cindy and Doug had to settle for a place on the edge. No cheerleaders here. Track and field was not a sport you revved people up for. They either went for it or they didn't. Or they were relatives.

Doug caught sight of his parents in the crowd and waved to them.

"What should I watch for?" Cindy, rather disoriented, asked Doug.

She had a good point. The meet was like a three-ring circus with different events taking place in different areas of the field.

"Nothing yet," Doug told her. If he had known things would be this slow, he would have taken more time at McDonald's with Cindy, maybe buy sundaes instead of cutting it short after the Big Macs.

"May I join you?" A woman's voice cut through his thoughts. Doug looked up. It was Mrs. Nathan, Willy's mother, still dressed in her business suit and heels. "Has the running started yet?"

"Not yet, I don't think. We just got here. Mrs. Nathan, I'd like you to meet Cindy Ballentine. Willy Nathan is one of the fastest runners Kennedy Junior High has," Doug explained to Cindy. "The team's won the last three meets. Willy's sure to make all-county.

"Look. It's the eight hundred, Kara's race. Number twenty-seven. Watch her run."

Cindy edged forward, then stood up because everyone else in this part of the bleachers stood up. She tried to keep her eye on Doug's sister, who was on her mark, getting set, and gone!

Doug was screaming encouragement, as if "Go, go go!" could make his sister travel any faster. "Second!" he shouted with disappointment as the runners crossed the finish line.

He sat down, and Cindy put her arm on his shoulder to comfort him. "She ran like a beautiful machine," she told him.

"That's what athletes are." He sounded like a commentator.

"Second, and she's only in seventh grade," Mrs. Nathan reminded him. "Now there's potential."

"What's next?" Cindy asked.

"Men's fifteen hundred, Willy's race."

"For his sake, I hope he wins," Mrs. Nathan said.

Doug could see her hands clutching her bag. "Don't worry, Mrs. Nathan. He could beat the field running backward. He won't lose."

But he almost did. An outside sprinter caught up to him on the final stretch, but Willy pulled ahead for a narrow victory.

Doug watched the board while they put up the

times. Then he turned to Mrs. Nathan and said, "He's going to make it to the Olympics one day."

"He hopes to," she confirmed with a tired smile.

"I ache just watching them," Cindy said. "It's nothing like the pom squad. It's so much more—well, real."

"A lot of pain included," Doug informed her. "And they're always worried about torn ligaments or pulled muscles."

"Not broken fingernails, I guess," she teased.

"Let's face it, Cindy, you were meant to buy your vegetables at the supermarket, that's all."

"How is your garden coming, Doug?" Mrs. Nathan asked.

Doug looked to Cindy and laughed. "I started working on it today. With Cindy's help."

"I still remember those tomatoes and peas you sent over with Willy last year. It's encouraged me to plant a garden myself. Someday I hope you'll come over and give me a little bit of advice."

"Sure, I'd be glad to, Mrs. Nathan."

"What are they doing now?" Cindy asked. "Why are the runners scattered all over the field?"

"It's the relays," Doug explained. "There's the Kennedy team in red. Kara's running third; Willy, the anchor."

The runners were stationed around the track. Then the gun sounded and the race was on. Doug had eyes only for his sister's team as the first runner passed to the second runner, then the second runner passed to Kara. Kara was running fast when she got the baton, running in her zone, her eyes squarely forward on Willy ahead of her.

Those in the stands watched Willy take off, perhaps a fraction too soon, perhaps a fraction too fast. Kara couldn't catch up with him, and he was almost at the point where he had to have the baton or be disqualified. Kara made a lunge toward him. Willy turned back like a wide receiver. The baton fell between them.

The crowd gasped.

Kennedy Junior High was disqualified in the relays.

"We have just seen the end of a beautiful friendship," Mrs. Nathan commented dryly. She stood up. "I think this calls for a massive dose of psychological first aid. But I do mean what I said before, Doug. I would love some advice on gardening. If you have the time to give it." She gave them a bright smile. Then she was gone, headed toward the field, toward Willy and Kara who were squaring off like bulldogs in a pit.

29

The Sunday afternoon that followed his Saturday date with Cindy felt strange to Doug, almost out of place and time. He spent most of the day out in his garden, debating exactly what Cindy had meant when she said, "This has been the most unusual date I've ever had."

He couldn't remember if she had smiled when she said it or not. He recalled they were both red and puffing after pedaling from Northwood to her house. Well, he would see on Monday. If she spoke to him again, then their date couldn't have been all that bad.

Maybe he shouldn't wait until Monday. Maybe he should just call and ask her what she had meant.

Which was why he was inside when Willy came over to apologize to Kara for calling her a stupid, dumb, ignorant lump who moved like an ox.

Kara tried to slam the door in his face, but it got stuck on his chest and his hipbone first. Doug was so long in trying to extricate Willy without getting his fingers smashed that he forgot to call Cindy. "You just need more practice, that's all," he told them, while

Kara raged on about Willy's grandstanding and lack of teamwork, and Willy protested innocently, "I didn't realize how slow you were."

In the end they grudgingly conceded to let the coach decide what, or more importantly who, had gone wrong.

All this while Mom and Dad were out somewhere in the countryside having a picnic. Doug was glad someone was having a good time.

Night came. Doug thought of Cindy. But she wasn't his only problem. He also thought of Red. He had spent a week avoiding Red, checking out hallways like a cornered animal before he raced down them to reach his next class. Going home immediately after school. Walking with his head down, his eyes averted. Why? He hadn't done anything. And yet here he was, the one acting like a criminal.

There had to be an end to this. Somewhere, sometime, he had to put it to rest.

Soon. Sooner.

He decided he would not spend another minute in an effort to keep out of Red's way. If they met, fine. He would face it. He couldn't run away forever.

He slept that night with this resolution. Monday morning he would have been in school at the usual time but the bus broke down with a flat tire. They had to walk the last half mile. When he got to school, almost everyone was in homeroom. He heard the P.A. announcing his late bus arrival, so he knew he wouldn't have to go to the office for a slip. He opened his locker and out fell a thin packet of sunflower seeds. "From your happy farmer," it said. "Guess who?" He smiled. So maybe Cindy liked the unusual after all.

It was funny, that week in school. Unlike last week, he walked down the corridors without flinching. Still he never met up with Red Bucknell. And he was annoyed by that, because sometimes he felt that this was where the answer lay for him. Meeting up with Red Bucknell. Slaying this dragon of his own making.

But it didn't happen until Thursday afternoon, when his whole gym class had been called in for a set of twenty push-ups. That was after they had fooled around and shot their volleyballs into the other side of the gym where the girls were jumping double Dutch.

When Doug came out of the gym entrance of the school, Red Bucknell was by the door. He wasn't alone. He was with several members of the football team, Charlie Sims among them.

Doug assumed it was coincidental. He prayed Red had not been waiting for him.

"Hi, Doug. How's it going?" Red said. Always original.

"Hello, Red," Doug answered somberly.

"Hey, have you been avoiding me?"

Doug could have answered either way. So he said nothing, just stood there looking from Red to his friends.

"I hear we're going to meet at the trial in June."

"That's what the state attorney's office tells me," Doug replied.

"So what are you going to say?"

"I'll answer the questions," Doug told him. Red's friends moved closer. Menacing him? But the lawyer, who had plotted everything so neatly, must have told Red it wouldn't look right if a promising young adult and his friends busted up the prosecution's chief witness.

"Like what sort of questions? About my condition? How do you know what condition I was in? You were drinking, too."

"One beer."

"One beer. You're fifteen. That's illegal."

"Not as illegal as killing three people."

"Hey, it was an accident!" Red exploded.

Doug nodded. "You're innocent until proven guilty." He started to walk away.

"Wimp," Red muttered, angrily wheeling up behind him.

Doug turned on him. "Tell me, Red, do you feel anything about those deaths?"

"What's to feel? It happened. It was an accident."

"Do you really believe that? Do you honestly think, if you hadn't been drinking, the *accident* would have happened?"

Red must have seen that Doug wasn't taunting him but was asking a real question. "I've been drinking and driving ever since I got my license," he said, making what to Doug was a dangerous admission. "I know how to hold my liquor. It was an accident, pure and simple. I just lost control of the car. It happens. Maybe the steering wheel was defective. Maybe the brakes."

"Maybe the driver." But Doug didn't say it out loud. "Did your attorney have the car checked out?"

"Yeah, he did. It was such a mess they couldn't find anything. But I know my limits. Do you think I would deliberately set out to kill someone?"

"No," Doug admitted. "I don't think you would."

"Hey, listen, let me ask you a question. If you thought I was so drunk that I couldn't drive, if you thought the others in the car with me were in such danger, why didn't you get them out along with you and Cindy?"

Doug sighed. "I have been asking myself that question ever since the hour I heard what happened," he said sadly.

"So what's the answer?"

"No answer. No excuse," Doug admitted. "I knew you were dead drunk; I knew you shouldn't drive. I knew you couldn't even stay on the road. I knew you were going to kill somebody. And yet I let you drive off with them."

"So maybe that makes *you* the murderer, huh?"

"Maybe." Doug faced it finally. "Maybe it does."

30

"Nonsense!" Mrs. Nathan spat the word out.

Doug had come there unannounced and unexpected.

It was the weekend, a long, lazy weekend. Doug had been out working on his garden, or trying to. Yet all he saw were the months slipping by him. He had pulled himself out of the well, had almost reached the top, and now he was afraid he was going to lose his hold and slide down again. It wasn't fair. He had to stop it from happening.

He didn't know how he had gotten to Willy's home. He didn't even know he knew which house was Willy's, all the houses on their streets looked so much alike. Mrs. Nathan had answered the door. She was like his mother—same age, same jeans, same way of not caring how she looked on a weekend.

"Hi, Mrs. Nathan. You said last Saturday you wanted to see me about your garden?"

"Ah! Yes. I'm glad to see you, Doug. I thought for a while we were going to have a real war on our hands, but I see Willy and Kara have made up."

"Well, they're running together again. But I don't

know if they have quite made up yet. "

"It's a start," she told him. "Hold on a second, now." She quickly grabbed a windbreaker from her closet, put it on, and led him around to the back of the house. It was a pleasant area: terraced and shaded, with a wood picnic table warped from years of weathering.

"Where do you think I should put it?" she asked.

"Put what?"

"My garden."

Doug looked up at the sunny sky, then down at her shaded lawn. "I thought you already had a garden."

"No. I'm thinking of starting one."

"Oh."

"What's your advice?"

"Don't put it back here. You don't get enough sun."

"Put it in the front yard and spoil my grass?"

He shrugged.

"Choices." She paused. "How's Red Bucknell?" she asked. A feinting move?

"What?" He was very articulate when he had to be.

"I have a friend connected with the state attorney's office. She said Red's back in school."

"Yes."

"How do you feel about his being back?"

He had seen enough shows about psychologists on television to know they always asked questions like that. It was a cliché. So why should he answer? "Embarrassed," he blurted out against his own defenses.

"Like you two shared a dirty secret?"

"Sort of," he agreed. He started talking then. He told her about his run-in with Red. That's when she burst out with the "Nonsense!"

"He doesn't feel guilty," Doug informed her.

"Has it ever occurred to you that he can't allow himself to feel guilty? That the enormity of what he has done doesn't allow him to face the act itself, even though society forces him to face its consequences? But you're not guilty."

"Oh, no."

"Oh, yes. That's why you can examine what happened, can sort and sift through the events of that night, can lay the blame on yourself for something you feel you should have done."

"Everyone says I did all that could have been expected of a fifteen-year-old boy."

"And you complete the rest of the thought by thinking that if you had been older, you would have done more?"

"Yes."

She shook her head. "Oh, Doug," she sighed. "Do you know that of all traffic accidents in this country, seventy-five to eighty percent are alcohol related? And some believe the percentage is higher."

He was startled.

"Yes," she agreed with him. "It is horrible—horrible precisely because these accidents are so preventable. By the very people who drink and drive. Not by the innocent bystanders. Which you were." She sounded convincing. "Just think of how many Dougs there are out there who say to themselves after the fact—if only."

He did think about it, but he rejected the comfort of numbers. "It doesn't help me, knowing there are others."

"Right," she agreed. "You still have to wonder, why you? Why you alone, with Cindy, got out of the car while the other three perished. The others did what we all do. They went along with what was happening because they thought they were invincible. Who, after all, would believe that death is coming down the highway toward them?"

"I did," Doug remembered.

"That was your gift, Doug."

"My gift?" he repeated grimly.

"Yes, your gift," she said firmly. "Because that's what life is." She smiled. "Do you remember what your mother always told you to say when you received a gift?"

Doug grimaced.

"I see you do. What was it?"

"To say thank you. Even if I didn't like it."

She nodded. "Most of us receive the gift of life only once, when we're born. We don't know it's a gift at the time. We just take a gulp of air and start breathing. You received the gift of life a second time, when you didn't stay in that car with Red Bucknell. And you know what you're doing wrong? Why you're having all these problems?"

"Why?"

"You forgot your manners. You forgot to accept the gift, to say thank you."

Doug stuck his hands in his pockets and stood stubbornly. "What if I don't think I deserve the gift?"

"That's the good thing about some gifts. They come to you without your asking. Now you're stuck with it. You've got to write your thank you note and make good use of it."

"So it's as simple as that? Accepting what happened as what happened?"

"And that nothing is ever going to change it," she said firmly. "It can't be altered. You can't wake up and find that it was only a dream, that it didn't happen. Because it did. And although part of your gift is the horrible gift wrapping, soon you'll be able to throw the wrapping away."

He looked at her. She seemed so confident, so sure, that he almost believed.

She smiled at him and he felt as if a big bandage had

covered all his wounds. He shifted uncomfortably. "You know, you really could have a decent garden in the front yard. Grass doesn't do anything for you except look green."

"Actually, I like to mow it," she confessed. "It gives me time to think when I mow the grass. But if you come up with any other brilliant ideas on where to put my garden, let me know."

31

Doug walked home, back to his own garden, and sank down next to the rows of peas he had planted two weeks ago. The green young stems were just now peeking above the earth, casting off their casings. Most of them. They stood like soldiers on parade. Except for a few vacant spots where the seeds had not sprouted. And here and there were yellow stems that would not grow right. He plucked them out without a thought and tossed them onto the grass to die.

Then it struck him that here he was with his pea patch, playing God. Yes, because, even as the seedlings grew, he would have to thin them out, pull out healthy ones to give the others space to grow, to bear fruit.

How horrible. That in his mind he had connected the act of gardening to the accident. As if God was thinning out—

Don't try to shift the blame, he warned himself. The blame—he looked into his conscience. He was not blameless in so many things. But he was not guilty, *not* guilty in the deaths of three human beings. The blame there lay squarely on Red Bucknell, who had chosen to drink and drive, oblivious to the consequences.

Doug lay back in the grass. The guilt that had haunted him since the day following the accident fled. He looked up at the sun and shielded his eyes. It dazzled him. Life was a gift.

Then the ground thundered under him. At first Doug thought an earthquake had come to Maryland. But no. It was just Willy and Kara circling through the backyard on their run around the development.

"Come on and join us," Kara called. "We'll hold down the pace."

He sat up. All of the sudden he felt like running. "Hey, I can keep up," he assured them.

"You'll never go the distance," Willy, a headband holding back his blond, curly hair, warned.

Doug smiled and accepted the challenge. "Just watch me."